Richmond upon Thames Libraries

Renew online at www.richmond.gov.uk/libraries

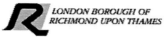

Look out for more in
The Ghost Hunter Chronicles series

The House in the Woods

THE RIPPER OF WHITECHAPEL

YVETTE FIELDING

ANDERSEN PRESS

First published in 2022 by
Andersen Press Limited
20 Vauxhall Bridge Road, London SW1V 2SA, UK
Vijverlaan 48, 3062 HL Rotterdam, Nederland
www.andersenpress.co.uk

2 4 6 8 10 9 7 5 3 1

British Library Cataloguing in Publication Data available.

ISBN 978 1 83913 214 8

Printed and bound in Great Britain by Clays Ltd, Elcograf S.p.A.

For my grandma Mary.

Always

PROLOGUE

Whitechapel, London, 1888

The excitement was bubbling up inside him. He hadn't been seen, he was sure of it. With his back against the grimy wall, he gingerly peeked round the corner. Through the foggy darkness he could just make out her muddy skirts swishing away from him.

Without losing sight of his prey, he slid along the brick wall, staring at her through half-closed wicked eyes. The woman suddenly stopped outside a battered old doorway and placed a key in the lock. She looked from left to right, making sure no one was following her. Once satisfied that it was safe to enter, she disappeared through the door.

If anyone were to see him, they would describe him as a gentleman. A smart top hat and black cloak hid his true identity from the suspicious eyes of Whitechapel.

He was hungry for his kill and this woman was next on the list. Licking his lips, he could almost taste the sweet delights of her blood. He shook his head and whispered to himself to calm down and wait for a while. After all, she wasn't going anywhere, was she?

Standing back in the dark, he observed the row of tiny houses and the flickering lights behind their dirty windows. Impoverished, stinking families, crowded together in foul, small hovels. It disgusted him to even think about it. Going into one of his victims' homes wasn't his preferred way of dealing with them, but he really liked this woman and knew that he had to enter her domain in order to do what needed to be done. He knew he would see the filth and despair, but he couldn't help himself. He wanted to kill her, he needed to kill her. A chortle rose up in his throat. He was pleased with himself, he was Jack the Lad, he was the Ripper. Telling himself he was his victims' saviour helped to justify his actions. He was saving these women's souls from living in such filth and squalor, wasn't he? He was their avenging angel, and Jack wasn't going to disappoint them.

Smiling to himself, he imagined the faces of the police when they discovered the latest corpse. Should he send another signed letter to Scotland Yard? Perhaps. He would decide later. They would never find him. He was too clever for them and they were far too stupid.

Jack knew it was time when the twinkling white candlelight from her window was extinguished. It was late; now was the moment to begin. He swallowed back the acid in his dry mouth and licked his mean, thin lips. Nerves and excitement made his stomach flip, he could feel his heart hammering in his chest.

Like a black, silent spectre, he glided up to the door and

picked the lock with his special knife. A little twist and satisfying click, and he was in.

The tiny room was dark except for the small glow left by the embers of a pathetic fire dying down in the grate. His victim's clothes were folded neatly on a wooden chair in the corner of the room. She was asleep, her long black hair falling over her face and down over the dirty pillow. He stood over her, smiling, like a cat that had cornered a mouse. Placing his gloved hands around her scrawny neck, he began to squeeze and squeeze, taking all the life from her. There was no struggle. It was easy and so wonderful. But just as he was about to plunge his long surgical blade into her warm flesh, the door creaked open, and two small children dressed in white nightgowns stared in horror at him.

They had seen his face! This would never do.

'Mama?' whispered one of them.

'Who are you?' said the other, a little louder. She walked forward, dragging a doll behind her.

The man in the top hat and long black cloak went to the children, smiling. In one swift move, he picked them up, huddled them inside his cloak and silently left the little hovel.

The children were never seen again.

CHAPTER 1

A Friend in Need

It was the first day of the summer holidays. The sun was beating down on Eve's back as she pedalled her bike towards Tom's house. She was excited to start the holidays off with her best mates Tom and Clovis — they had so much to fit in. As she rode the short distance from her own house, she wondered which item on their busy schedule they would do first: the cinema, swimming or the theme parks? But really she knew which one they would all be most *excited* to do. Ghost hunting. Ghost hunting was their passion, and the friends had really begun to take this unusual hobby very seriously — helped by Eve's strange and rather eccentric Uncle Rufus, of course.

Eve and her friends had first stepped into the world of the paranormal last Halloween and now they were desperate for more spooky adventures. For the last few months, Uncle Rufus had been teaching them about the world of the supernatural and all the famous cases, as well as showing them how to use many of the ghost-hunting devices he'd invented. But now the friends were eager to take what they had learned out into the world. Eve had decided that tonight, when she got back home, she would talk to her uncle about the possibility of the three of them going with him on his next proper investigation.

Eve squeezed the brakes on her bike as she rode up to Tom's house, leaned her bike up against the wall and knocked on the door. It wasn't long before Tom's dad's huge outline could be seen through the frosted glass. He opened the door, the chain dangling across his bulbous face as he glared through the small gap.

'Oh, hello, Mr Lake. I've come for Tom.'

Tom's dad grunted, unhooked the chain and opened the door fully. He wiped his hands down the front of his stained white vest and nodded upwards, indicating that his son was upstairs in his room.

Eve had never seen Tom's dad smile, not once in all the years she had known the family. She knew how Tom felt about him and how upset he got over the way his dad treated his mum, Ange. They were always arguing, and his dad often barked orders at Tom's mum, who nervously did his bidding.

Eve smiled brightly at Mr Lake, hoping to encourage some sort of happy response, but as usual, no luck.

'Go on up,' he grunted over the sound of the TV. He shuffled his large body around and, without a backwards glance, went into the front room to carry on watching his programme.

Eve ran up the stairs two at a time and knocked on Tom's door. 'Hey, it's me. You ready?' No response.

'Tom?' She knocked again, harder this time. She was just about to knock a third time, when she heard a small voice.

'Come in.'

Eve pushed the door open, just a little, and peeked through into Tom's tiny bedroom. Her friend was sitting on the floor, his back against the side of his bed, staring sadly into space. Something was wrong.

'Hey, what's up?' Eve sat down next to him and leaned in close. Tom was always the happy one in their group, the one who liked to see the positive side of things. What had happened to make him look like this?

Tom didn't respond at first, he just stared at the floor. Then Eve noticed his chin begin to wobble.

'Mum's gone.' The statement was delivered quietly, almost a whisper. He turned to face Eve and only then did she see just how upset he was. His face was tear-stained, eyes red and swollen.

'Gone where? . . . What, she's *left*? Oh my God! Tom, I'm so sorry. When did this happen?' Eve grasped her best friend's hand, squeezing it tight.

'This morning. I woke up and heard them rowing again, but this time it was different. My mum was the one doing the shouting. She said if he didn't change his ways, she would leave for good. Then she came upstairs, kissed me and said she'd be back for me soon. She's gone to my auntie's house in Leeds.' Tom paused and let out a long breath. He pulled a loose red thread that had come away from the old rug on the floor, winding it round and round his finger, staring at it intently as if the thread itself were the cause of his upset. 'She says she's going to sort a place for us up there and then she's coming back for me.' Tom sniffed and wiped his watery eyes with the back of his hand. 'I want her here with *me*. I miss her so much already and I don't want to be stuck in the house with *him*.' His voice began to falter with emotion.

Tom sucked in a long breath, trying to mentally calm himself down. He squeezed his eyes tight shut, and then whispered, 'And I don't want to live in bloody Leeds.'

Eve put her arm round his shoulders. She wanted to make the hurt go away. She knew how close Tom and his mum were. He did so much to help her and she was always the parent he could turn to. They had each other's back. Tom had been able to cope with his dad's moods because he always knew he had his mum. But now she was gone. Eve didn't know what to say. She squeezed his shoulder. 'It'll be all right, you'll see. Your mum will be back soon and I bet she changes her mind about Leeds.'

'D'you think so?'

'Definitely.' Eve swallowed her true thoughts and fears. She couldn't bear it if Tom moved away. Tom and Clovis were her best friends, her only friends, really. Sure, she knew other girls and messed about with them at school but Clovis and Tom were her true friends.

'Come on,' said Eve, trying to sound upbeat and happy. She sprang up and began to pull at Tom's arm. 'Come and stay with me and Uncle Rufus. You might as well, until your mum comes back.' Eve certainly wasn't going to leave Tom here with his dad. He would end up doing all the cooking and chores, and have to put up with the moods. No, Eve wasn't having that. No way. He could stay at her house. She knew how much Tom loved Professor Rufus and that her uncle would be happy for him to stay.

'Are you sure the professor won't mind?'

'Course I'm sure, he'll love it. He'll have more people to tell ghost stories to.'

It worked. Tom got up, grabbed a bag from the top of his wardrobe and began to stuff clothes into it.

'I'll have to ask . . . *him.*' He said the word 'him' as if spitting out a disgusting piece of food. 'But I'm sure he'll be OK with it. It's not as if he's going to miss me, is it?'

After Tom and Eve had packed as much as they could into the bag, they made their way down to the front room.

Dan Lake was wedged into his well-worn armchair, the TV blaring out. The main horserace was on and Dad was fully absorbed by it. He sat upright, bouncing up and down in the small armchair and shouting as if the horse he had backed could hear him. 'Go on, Peggy's Legs, get a bloody move on!' Dad yelled; his eyes gleamed with excitement.

Tom looked on and thought how sad it was that his dad showed more enthusiasm for a horse he didn't know than for him and his mum.

Dad hadn't always been this way though. According to Mum, he'd been a happy man, besotted and totally in love with her. Apparently, he couldn't wait to have a son so he could play with him, read to him, take him to football matches. Tom had seen all the photographs of his parents when they were younger — laughing, dancing and sunbathing on the beach. And the old videos of his dad chasing his mum around the garden, spraying her with the hose as she squealed with delight. But then it all changed, the war came in Afghanistan and his soldier dad was shipped off. And when he came home, he just wasn't the same. He was quiet, sullen most of the time, except when his explosive rages would appear from nowhere. Tom remembered being so scared one night that he ran upstairs to hide under his bed until his mum found him, put him under the duvet and held him tight. His mum was always trying to explain that his dad was a good man really, but he was damaged and hurt by a terrible war that had killed many of his best friends. Tom knew there had been another side to his dad, a fun side, a happy side, a side that loved him, he just wished he could see it. Was it too late? Tom definitely thought so and it seemed now so did his mum.

'Dad?' shouted Tom above the din.

Dad's eyes were glued to the television. He didn't move

a muscle and answered back curtly, annoyed at the interruption. 'What?'

'Can I go and stay with Eve for a bit?'

'How long for?' Still Dad's eyes didn't leave the screen.

'Just for a few days.'

'Suppose,' Dad shouted back over the din. The racing was obviously coming to its finale, the commentator's voice was at an excitable pitch, ridiculous horse names spewed out of the TV one after the other.

'Great, thanks, Dad,' said Tom. His stomach flipped over, the familiar feeling of relief washed over his body.

'Get your uncle to call me,' shouted Dad to Eve, now on the edge of his seat.

'Will do,' said Eve.

Tom was already pushing her out of the door, he didn't want to hang about.

The race obviously came to a disappointing conclusion for Dad. Tom and Eve could hear the swearing as they left the house.

'Quick,' said Tom, straddling his bike. 'Before he changes his mind.'

'Let's go and get Clovis,' shouted Eve over her shoulder as they set off pedalling.

The three friends all lived on the same estate and had grown up together. Tom lived in a small council house, Clovis in a flat with his mum and older brother Jahmeel, and Eve lived in the weirdest house in the area with her eccentric

Uncle Rufus. Eve's house was very old and positioned between two council tower blocks, one of which Clovis and his family lived in. The ancient house, with its crooked walls and warped black and white timber beams, looked as if the life was being squeezed out of it by the tower blocks that hugged it from either side.

'I hope Clovis's mum has made one of her cakes,' called out Eve as she bumped her bike down a kerb.

Tom's face lit up at the thought, obviously the situation at home had been put to the back of his mind and Claudette's cake was now at the forefront. 'Fingers crossed it's the chocolate one,' he said, licking his lips and smiling.

The pair cycled the short journey to Clovis's tower block. Much to their annoyance the lifts were out of action again so they both sighed, rolled their eyes and reluctantly hitched their bikes up onto their shoulders to begin the long trek up the stairs. Once on Clovis's floor, Tom and Eve walked slowly, panting to catch their breaths. They leaned their bikes up against the railings opposite Clovis's front door and Tom rang the doorbell.

Jahmeel, Clovis's older brother, answered. 'Hiya, come in. He's in the kitchen with Mum. Clovis!' he called out. 'It's your girlfriends!'

Eve playfully punched Jahmeel on the arm while Tom flicked the back of his head.

The smell of a freshly baked cake wafted under everyone's noses. In the small kitchen, Clovis was sitting at the table, stuffing his face with the squidgiest-looking chocolate cake Tom had ever seen. Claudette Gayle was resting against the fridge with a large mug of something in her hands. Her face lit up when she saw Eve and Tom.

'Well, hello, you two. Cake? As if I need to ask,' she chortled as she cut two massive slices, placed them on plates and put them on the kitchen table. 'Sit,' she commanded warmly. 'And I want it all eaten.'

Clovis mumbled a familiar 'Hey' to Tom and Eve through his mouthful of cake.

'Do you want to come back to mine?' asked Eve. 'Thought we could watch a movie and have a pizza tonight.'

Clovis nodded happily while shovelling more cake into his mouth. It always astounded Eve that he could eat so much and remain so slim. And at almost six feet tall, with his dark skin and Afro hair, he was striking; lots of girls at school thought so. Of course Clovis wasn't interested in good looks or fashion or even girls, all he cared about was researching facts and periods of history. He looked super-intelligent too, with his large square glasses that were for ever steaming up, a sign that he was excited about some fact which most people would find boring.

Eve began to rib him about the latest girl at school who seemed to have taken a shine to him. Jahmeel joined in and the three of them happily joked and teased each other.

Claudette took the opportunity to sit down next to Tom. She took his hand in hers and leaned in close. 'I spoke with your mother this morning, she told me to keep an eye out for you . . . are you OK, darlin'?' she whispered.

'Yeah, I'll be fine.' Tom looked uncomfortably down at his feet, hoping Claudette would understand that he didn't want to talk about it.

'Your mum told me she's just taking a little holiday.' Claudette carried on rubbing Tom's hand in hers as she spoke. Tom blanked out her voice, so that it sounded like a soft drone in the background. He looked down at his feet, noticing the different marks and stains on his Converse trainers. Hot tears burned in his eyes. He blinked them away quickly, desperate that no one should see how upset he was.

He tuned back in to Claudette's voice. '. . . I'm sure she'll be back in a few days and everything will go back to normal real soon.' Then she grabbed Tom and hugged him to her. He squeezed his eyes tight, swallowing down his embarrassment and momentarily enjoyed the comforting smell of rose talc and cake.

Claudette gently let Tom go from her embrace. 'You can stay here with us if you like.'

'Thanks, Claudette, but I'm going to stay with Eve and the professor.'

'Well, I'm always here for you, Tom. You know that don't you, darlin'?' Claudette got up from the table, her colourful chunky necklaces clanking and jangling against each other.

'Thank you. I know that.' Tom smiled and got up to kiss Claudette on the cheek. She ruffled his blond locks.

'When you going to get that mop cut, young man?'

Clovis decided to come to his friend's rescue. 'Mum, thanks for the cake, can we go now?'

'Can Clovis stay at mine?' asked Eve, giving one of her most persuasive looks.

'Yes. OK then,' laughed Claudette. 'Remember to brush your teeth, young man.'

'Yes, Mum, I will,' answered Clovis, feeling a little self-conscious. 'Come on, guys, let's go.'

Once out into the hot afternoon sun, they rode their bikes through the estate and up into the nearby park. By the shade of a lone oak tree, they sat in the long grass, looking down on the city of London.

'I'm so excited,' sighed Eve. She lay back, the grass tickling her pale freckled skin as she watched the few wisps of white cloud float over their heads.

'What about?' asked Clovis.

'This summer. I've a funny feeling we're going to have another adventure.'

'That would be brilliant!' said Tom. 'I could do with that.'

'I'm going to ask Unc if we can go on a real ghost hunt. Maybe even by ourselves. I think we're ready, don't you? We've done loads of case studies and understand how to use most of the ghost-hunting equipment now.' Eve sat up and ran her fingers through her short spiky blonde hair. The boys were reminded of an adventurous pixie that could never sit still for long. Tom and Clovis loved her like a sister and were extremely protective of her. She was the one who always came up with the schemes and plans that, more times than not, landed them in trouble.

'Here we go again,' said Tom.

'I think we could give it a go,' said Clovis, looking at Tom knowingly, 'but I'd prefer it if the professor came too. Last time we tried to ghost hunt on our own, we brought a distressed spirit home with us. I don't want to put my family through that again.'

'Yeah, I agree,' said Tom.

'Oh, all right,' said Eve, 'I guess you've got a point. I'll ask him.' She suddenly jumped up and raced to her bike. 'Last one to the Pizza Palace has to pay!' She began to pedal down the hill furiously.

'Eve!' shouted back Tom and Clovis, scrambling behind and trying to catch up.

CHAPTER 2

Mr Wilson has a Terrible Fright

Mr Wilson, the deputy headteacher of Whitechapel Primary School, was going through some last-minute paperwork before he left the building for his summer holidays. He would be glad to get away. The new building works had been a nightmare. The parents' committee had paid for a new wing to be built on the end of the old school. The workmen had only been digging and building for about a week, but it seemed like an age. The drilling and banging had driven all the teachers mad with frustration and the children's concentration had been somewhat compromised. By the time they all came back from their summer break, hopefully the new wing would be finished and all could go back to normal again.

He was really looking forward to this holiday; he and his family were going away for a much-needed trip to Spain. He closed his eyes briefly, shut out the sights and smells of his musty old office, and imagined himself lying in the sun. He gave a deep sigh, relishing the action of locking his desk for the last time this term. But as he stood and reached for his bag, he heard a child giggling in the distance. *How odd*. All the children had left for their summer break yesterday. There should be no one here but himself. Swinging his bag over his shoulder, Mr Wilson peeked out into the corridor and listened. Nothing.

Thinking he must have imagined it, he locked up his office and strode purposefully towards the exit. Suddenly, he stopped in his tracks. At the end of the corridor, he could see two children running.

'Hey!' he shouted.

There was no response. Mr Wilson was now convinced that there *were* children messing about inside the school. When he caught whoever it was, there was going to be trouble, that was for sure. He walked quickly in the direction of the children. When he reached the end of the corridor and turned the corner, he was expecting to see them.

He saw nothing, but he could *hear* the voices of two children. One was giggling, the other was singing.

> *Ring-a-ring o' roses,*
> *A pocket full of posies;*
> *A-tishoo, a-tishoo,*
> *We all fall down ...*

Mr Wilson followed the sweet singing voice, and entered a classroom.

'Right, what are you two doing here? You shouldn't

be . . .' Mr Wilson's booming voice faded into nothing, his mouth began to open and close like a stranded goldfish. He didn't recognise them. They certainly didn't go to this school. They were dressed bizarrely, and one of them was rocking backwards and forwards in the corner of the room. Mr Wilson was unnerved. Suddenly fear gripped him, twisting his stomach into a tight knot. Something was very wrong with these two kids.

Standing in the centre of the room was a girl, about eight years old. She was wearing a white nightgown and her long black hair fell about her face like a pair of wet curtains. Her skin was white as snow but her eyes were black and deep. She looked as if she had been swimming, because all around her bare feet rippled a puddle of murky dark water. In her small white hand, she held a bedraggled-looking doll — it was also sodden. The other child in the corner was younger, about three or four years old, a boy, but also dressed in a long white nightgown. He too looked to be soaked to the skin.

Mr Wilson stumbled backwards in shock. He didn't know what to make of the scene unfolding before his eyes. He was an intelligent, logical man, who didn't believe in paranormal nonsense, but somehow he felt unnerved by the sight of these two children.

'Who are you?' he stammered, not quite sure he wanted to hear the answer. The children didn't reply, but the girl snapped her head up unnaturally and stared straight at him.

That look took Mr Wilson's breath away; for the first time in his life he felt nothing but pure dread. Something wasn't right.

The atmosphere in the classroom was awful, freezing. A sense of foreboding punched him in the chest, making his heart hammer like a train running at full speed. Shaking his head in confusion, Mr Wilson tried to make sense of what was happening. He drew himself up to his full height and took a deep breath, desperate not to let this awful feeling get the better of him.

The girl turned and walked very slowly towards him. Then in a flash she had moved at a speed that wasn't humanly possible and was standing an inch away from him. Her face flickered, as if she were an image in an old black and white movie, crackling in and out of vision. She looked all over the teacher's face, as if taking in every inch of him. He stood frozen in shock and horror.

Now the little boy crawled slowly across the floor in a jerky, erratic manner, even more unnerving than the staring girl. Any courage Mr Wilson had was fading rapidly. He knew these children were not natural, not of this world. Shaking and sweating, he cleared his throat and decided that he would try to talk to them.

'What do you want?' he shouted. His stomach flipped over, dreading a response. The girl moved her head to one side and blinked those large eyes slowly; the little boy stood up and seemed to glide quite effortlessly towards him. He came to a standstill next to the girl and took her hand in his. There they stood, all in white, looking like they had just been pulled out of a river. The girl began to speak. Her tiny mouth worked slowly, trying to form words that Mr Wilson couldn't hear. No sound came from the children, it was as if they were trapped in some sort of bubble where they couldn't be heard. And yet he had just heard her singing, hadn't he?

He suddenly remembered Mrs Kirby, his Year Three teacher, standing in his office just last week, shaking, crying and full of fear. She had said that she didn't like the building, that she'd seen something terrible that petrified her. She had described two figures dressed in white that were not of this world. Oh, how he and his colleagues had giggled and sniggered quietly behind their newspapers and sandwiches in the staffroom. The woman was mad, surely? With a guilty knot in his stomach, he now realised her bizarre ghost story was real: spirits that Mr Wilson had only ever read about or seen in horror movies were standing right in front of him, staring him squarely in the face.

Mr Wilson realised he was freezing cold, and was shocked to see his own breath as swirls of grey mist, floating away from him. The children still hadn't moved, and continued to stare intently at him.

Mr Wilson tried one more time to communicate. Slowly and carefully, he brought his hand up and moved it closer to the children. He needed to know if they were solid. They certainly didn't look it. They seemed half in this world and half in another dimension.

Just as his hand was about to touch the top of the boy's head, the girl's face suddenly exploded into rage. She mouthed words furiously and brought her fists up, trying to hit the teacher. But Mr Wilson didn't feel a thing, only an icy blast of air hitting his legs again and again. Then suddenly the children turned, startled by something. They looked behind them and Mr Wilson watched in horror as they began to scream. They had seen something that he couldn't, and it caused them so much fear. The girl turned and grabbed the little boy, and the teacher watched as the apparitions began to fade away. They were running, running for their lives. But from what?

Just as Mr Wilson thought his nightmarish ordeal was over, a large, dark shadow suddenly appeared. Mr Wilson stumbled backwards, trying to keep his balance. He put his arm out to one of the shelves that lined the walls but missed and fell. The black mass changed shape, swirling like a mist of thick, inky cobwebs. The shadowy figure became clearer: it was a man, but no ordinary man. His face was vile and putrid. The skin stretched across his skeletal features was sickly grey and mottled. His evil deep-set eyes were like red-hot coals, blazing with anger. He wore a black cloak and top hat.

Closer and closer he came, not quite solid, the smell horrific, thick sulphurous fumes permeating the classroom. Mr Wilson choked and gagged with the noxious gas. The teacher recoiled in horror, curling his body up as tight as he could. He began to shake violently, not just with abject fear but with the freezing cold. The temperature had dropped even more: Mr Wilson could see the windows had all iced up with white glittery frost inside the classroom. How bizarre, the teacher thought. The ghost's movements brought him out of his reverie and in that moment he resigned himself to the fact he was about to feel pain. Mr Wilson looked on in wide-eyed terror as the ghost opened a black bag and took out a long silver rod. The ghost's mouth suddenly and incomprehensibly started to open, and it kept opening, wider and wider, so much so that the poor teacher thought he was going to be devoured. Then Mr Wilson did feel the pain. The burning was so intense, he couldn't cope any more, his body and mind shut down, and he passed out.

When Mr Wilson came round, his vision was a blur, and tears were streaming down his face. Mr Ford, the caretaker, and a paramedic were bending over him, asking if he was OK. He screamed, terrified they were going to hurt him.

Mr Wilson never did go to Spain on his long-awaited holiday.

CHAPTER 3

A Call from the Inspector

Eve's house was a welcome sight for Tom. He'd loved it from the first time he ever called for Eve when they were at primary school together. Now they were thirteen, and many happy years had been spent in this ancient quirky building. The place had always felt like a second home to him. Its uneven floors and twisting staircases looked a bit creepy at first sight, but the more he visited, the more comfortable he'd felt.

Uncle Rufus, or 'the professor' as Tom and Clovis liked to call him, was a hero in their eyes. Yes, some people in the neighbourhood thought him a little strange, but that was because they didn't know him. He was a professor at one of the universities in the city. He loved his work but in his spare time he was obsessed with anything to do with the paranormal. It came from seeing his dead wife, Eve's aunt, a few years back. Since then he had been inventing ghost-hunting machines in the hopes of seeing her again. Eve had lost her parents in the same train crash as the professor's wife, and had been taken in by her Uncle Rufus as a young child. He had become something of a father to her.

Eve broke Tom's reverie as she rushed past him on the stone steps. 'Let's go and tell Unc that you're coming to stay.' She put her key into the massive oak door and pushed it open. Instantly Boris the bulldog sauntered towards them, sniffing, dribbling and snuffling.

'Argh, Boris,' laughed Clovis, patting the dog's huge head with one hand and balancing the pizza boxes with the other.

'Knickers!' The word was squawked loudly from the front room, and sure enough, Mr Pig the parrot came and settled on Eve's shoulder in a flurry of feathers and a beating of colourful wings.

'That's a new word,' laughed Tom.

'I know, I don't know where he's picked it up from,' answered Eve, looking guilty. She stroked the bright feathers of the exotic bird and he responded by quickly bobbing up and down — a sign that he was excited. Mr Pig had once been owned by a foul-mouthed sea captain, hence the bad language. He had then ended up as a companion for many years to an old friend of Uncle Rufus's, Jane Bains. Sadly, the old lady had died and Mr Pig had been kindly gifted to Eve and Uncle Rufus.

'His vocabulary is just getting worse. I think he picks rude words up off the telly and radio,' said Eve, blushing. Mr Pig was now shaking with sheer delight at all the attention he was receiving. 'Come on, Uncle Rufus will be up in his attic,' she said, placing Mr Pig on his stand in the front room.

'You arse!' screeched the parrot. Obviously he was not

happy at being put back on his perch and he began to bob up and down again, swearing outrageously at Eve. Clovis and Tom were in hysterics. Boris began to turn in circles, his little bottom wiggling excitedly.

'Watch this,' said Eve, grinning. She went over to the radio and pressed a button on the top of the speaker. Immediately the angry noise of thrash metal belted out around the room. Amazingly, Mr Pig opened his wings and began to head bang in time to the music.

Eve turned the radio off and produced a small biscuit from her pocket.

'Can you believe that a parrot would love thrash metal? He's crazy,' said Eve affectionately. She stroked Mr Pig's head gently and gave him the small biscuit.

Boris jumped up, sniffing out the tasty morsel. 'Oh, and you get one too.' Eve pulled out another little biscuit and gave it to a slobbering Boris, who showed his appreciation by letting out a very loud, thunderous fart.

'Boris!' cried Tom.

'That dog should come with his own health warning,' said Clovis, holding his nose.

'Come on. Let's go find Uncle,' said Eve happily.

They ran up the twisting, uneven staircase until they reached the top of the building, where they knocked quietly at the door and waited to be told to enter. They couldn't just walk in, that would be considered a heinous crime. No, they knew they'd have to wait to be invited into Uncle Rufus's attic, something that a while back none of them had ever thought possible.

Until recently Uncle Rufus's attic had been a complete mystery, a sacred place where only he was allowed. For years Tom, Clovis and Eve had seen all manner of strange objects going in and very rarely seen them coming out. It was a mysterious room where strange noises and voices were heard whispering out in the middle of the night. They had all tried to guess what went on in his attic but had never come to one solid conclusion.

Was he inventing machines for the government? Was he a spy? Was he building a spacecraft? Clovis and the others hadn't been able to believe their luck when one day Uncle Rufus invited them all upstairs to the top of the house and into his secret hideaway. It wasn't because he was feeling charitable or thoughtful. He had been furious with them all after discovering they'd gone to an old abandoned house and experimented with a Ouija board there. Because in doing so, they had unwittingly brought a very angry ghost back with them. Once the teenagers had come clean, Uncle Rufus had had to step in to help, and to do so he had taken them up into his attic and revealed his secret. He was a ghost hunter, an investigator of the paranormal. To their delight and wonder, he had shown them his ghost machines, shared his knowledge and brought each of them into the spooky, strange and secret world of the paranormal.

The machines he had were incredible. They had been

made to communicate with the dead. In fact, the professor was quite an expert on the subject and for the last few months he had been teaching the children everything he knew.

As they waited for a response to their tentative knock at the attic door, they could hear Uncle Rufus's voice coming from within. He was obviously on the phone to someone. Never ones to eavesdrop, Eve, Clovis and Tom were about to turn around. Eve whispered to the others that they should come back later, when suddenly they heard Uncle Rufus's voice begin to take on a rather more serious tone and they realised he was talking about *them*.

'Eve, Clovis and Tom? Yes, that's right . . . I think they're ready, absolutely . . . definitely! But this new case, well, I don't want them placed in any danger. No . . . I know you wouldn't, after all they are still just kids. Yes, all right. Yes . . . yes, I look forward to it.'

Eve, Tom and Clovis all looked quizzically at each other. Uncle Rufus was obviously talking about them, but who to and what about?

They each leaned closer to the door, trying to hear more of the strange conversation.

'All right, then, I'll bring them by tomorrow. Yes, I won't be late. Bye.'

The door suddenly flew open and everyone fell forward into the attic.

'Come in!' said Uncle Rufus sarcastically. Eve could tell he was trying not to laugh at their comical entrance.

Uncle Rufus was looking smart, as usual. He wore a shirt and tie no matter what. It was a hot day and most people were wearing T-shirts and shorts. But not Uncle Rufus. He had rolled up his shirt sleeves and for extra comfort had undone the top button of his shirt. Even on the hottest days, he was never without his trusty patched blue cardigan. Today it was lying across the back of his battered old sofa. Eve guessed her beloved aunt had knitted it. It was one of his most treasured possessions and he always panicked if he couldn't find it.

Uncle Rufus smiled at them. His brown hair was greying slightly and he ran his hand through his long unruly fringe, raking it away from his face and his old-fashioned spectacles. He sat down on the edge of the sofa. His inventions, some finished, others not quite, littered every space and corner. The biggest invention, and possibly the best, was Messenger One. This was the machine that converted the voices of the dead, which no human ear could hear, into the recognisable sounds of speech. It was an extraordinary piece of equipment that the professor had constructed out of an old copper bath, lots of copper wiring, a heating element and many trumpet horns.

Clovis looked at the machine sitting in the corner and smiled at it fondly. It was a marvellous piece of kit that had revealed to them all the voices of the spirits they had investigated in the autumn. It had blown their minds. He wondered what inventions the professor was working on at the moment, and looked around the room, hoping to find a clue. But all he saw was what looked to be a lot of jumble. Old telephones, telescopes, clocks, record players, trumpets, plastic human and animal heads, jars of strange, luminous liquids and all sizes of glass test tubes lined the walls, while lots and lots of colourful electrical wires protruded out of every drawer and cupboard.

Clovis looked up at the professor's ceiling. It was stunning. He had recreated all the constellations. The professor had said it helped him to concentrate and relax. Clovis could see why, and sighed deeply as Orion twinkled down on him.

'Well, now,' said the professor, taking off the pair of half-moon-shaped glasses. 'It seems we are all wanted at Detective Inspector Rutherford's headquarters tomorrow.'

Tom looked worried. 'Oh no, why?' he asked Uncle Rufus. 'Are we in trouble?' He remembered the last time they had encountered the strange lady police inspector; she had come to Eve's house after their previous ghostly adventure. They had thought they would all be in trouble with the police for entering the old abandoned house in the middle of Epping Forest. But then, they'd got the shock of their lives when Detective Inspector Rutherford seemed to know so much about the paranormal and was clearly excited about their findings. Maybe the inspector had changed her mind and was going to reprimand them.

'No, not at all,' chuckled Uncle Rufus. 'She wants to show you where she works.'

Tom expelled a huge sigh of relief.

'But why?' asked Eve, looking confused. 'It's just a police station, isn't it?'

'Well, that's just it. It's not *just* a police station. I think you'll find it very interesting. Aaaaand . . .' Uncle Rufus stretched out the word, then paused, smiling at them all. He leaned forward, eyes sparkling. Everyone waited, uncertain about what he was going to say. 'I think she wants your involvement with a new case that's just come in,' he said quickly. 'So, tomorrow I'm taking you to meet her at the headquarters of the Society of Paranormal Investigations, or SPI for short.' He closed his eyes, knowing the reaction would be an excitable one.

'Yes!' Eve punched the air, her face shining, brimming with joy.

Tom looked happy, though a little worried, and Clovis was elated, his face beaming.

'Oh my God! That's brilliant,' said Eve, bursting with excitement. 'I knew there was something going on with the inspector.'

'It's fantastic, Professor. I can't wait, but I hope . . .' Tom lowered his voice: '. . . it's not too dangerous.' Always the more careful and worried of the three friends, Tom was brave when he had to be, but after their last experience with ghosts and poltergeists, he didn't mind admitting he had been scared witless.

'So, does that mean you're part of this . . .' Eve tried to

remember the name of the society 'S . . . P . . . thingy? Is that how you met the inspector?' she added, rounding on her uncle.

'SPI,' added Clovis confidently.

'Yes, SPI,' continued Eve. 'Is that why you've been training us so much? Oh my God, can we become members?'

'Steady on,' laughed Uncle Rufus. 'Yes, Eve, I am a member and, yes, that is how I met the inspector.' He answered her questions with a smile, but there was a note of caution in his voice too. 'Listen, I would love nothing more than for you all to become part of the society eventually. I think it would be really good for you, and the organisation could benefit from some new blood. The inspector, I know for a fact, is keen for you to join now after all the training I've been giving you, but I'm a little more reluctant. I think you might need more time, more experience. I know you're very capable and brave and you all proved yourselves in the last case. But I've seen so many investigators who I thought were lifers, who ended up leaving because the fear got the better of them.' Uncle Rufus looked at the three crestfallen faces. He took a deep breath, ran his hand through his hair and gave them some hope. 'I'll tell you what, let me get all the facts about the case she wants investigating tomorrow and then let's talk about it.'

The three friends seemed happy with the little glimmer of hope that Uncle Rufus had just given them, and instantly began to chatter loudly with renewed excitement.

'Do you know what the case is, Professor?' asked Clovis, wanting to know as much information as possible.

'And is it dangerous?' asked Tom.

Eve was pacing the floor and gesticulating wildly. 'What time are we going and where is it? What should we wear?' She was planning in her head but talking out loud.

'All I know is the inspector would like to show you around the headquarters tomorrow, she thought it would be good for you to see where she works and to get your thoughts on a new haunting that she's been made aware of. That's as far as it goes for now.'

Then Uncle Rufus interrupted their excited chatter and eager preparations with a side-step of a question: 'Do I smell pizza?'

CHAPTER 4

A Guardian and an Old Tube Station

It was another hot sunny morning and after an exciting night of chatter, laughter and plenty of food, Uncle Rufus and the teenagers took the bus into Central London. During the half-hour journey, Uncle Rufus whispered about the upmost importance of total secrecy and how, if any of them spoke of what they were about to see, they would be in big trouble. Then he ushered the excited threesome off the bus and onto the busy streets of Aldwych. They bustled through the throngs of people who were each weaving in and out, concerned about nothing but themselves and where they were going. Eve, Tom and Clovis side-stepped and dodged early morning shoppers, joggers and people talking loudly on their phones. They kept an eye on Uncle Rufus's straw trilby hat, which bounced up and down just ahead of them.

Before long he started to slow down and glance cautiously about him. He seemed to be checking that they weren't being followed. Across the road, Uncle Rufus noticed a man on his phone who seemed to be looking straight at them.

'Is everything OK, Professor?' asked Clovis.

Straining his eyes, Uncle Rufus tried to get a better look, but it was useless, the sun was too bright and its rays dazzled him. The man jogged away quickly, dissolving into the busy crowds. Uncle Rufus craned his neck to see if he could find him again, but he had gone. The friends shared concerned looks. Had he been watching them? Or was Uncle Rufus just being paranoid?

Now the professor was standing with his back to the door of a building it seemed they were about to enter. He waited for the others to join him and, once he was satisfied that neither the man nor anyone else was watching, he urged the others to follow him quickly inside.

They had walked through the main entrance of what looked to be an old tube station. Its name was still on a large sign above the door: *STRAND STATION*, but it felt as though they had stepped back in time.

The air changed immediately. It was cool and slightly damp, a complete contrast to the warmth outside. The door shut loudly behind them, causing an eerie echo. The light was dim but they could just make out that they were standing in a big empty space. Eve, Tom and Clovis realised they were in a huge ticket hall that had obviously remained untouched for many years. An old-fashioned ticket office hugged the left-hand side of the old concourse, its wooden windows and door all boarded up. A sign remained on the wall, directing people to the *Tickets and Trains*, and a bit further down were several separate cupboard-like compartments, above which an old-fashioned sign read *Telephones,* though on closer inspection no telephones were inside. Diagonally opposite was a set of concrete steps leading down into a chasm of darkness.

'Wow!' cried Clovis. 'It's like we've travelled back in time.' A huge grin spread across his face. This was just the sort of place Clovis loved.

'Are we going down there?' asked Tom, looking a little nervously at the steps.

Uncle Rufus flicked a switch on the wall and instantly all the overhead lights danced on reassuringly. 'Come on,' he laughed, 'follow me. There are lights on most of the way.'

They now walked along cavernous corridors that seemed to go on for miles. White tiles lined arched walls which stretched on and on. Eventually a long steep flight of steps lay ahead, a metal handrail running down the middle. Uncle Rufus jogged down them, and at the very bottom, he looked back up, smiling.

'How far does this go?' asked Eve, more to herself than anyone else.

'Not far now,' called back her uncle. 'Come on, we're nearly there.'

Another long corridor loomed before them. It was more of a tunnel really, thought Tom, and he was secretly grateful that all the lights were on. On the tiled walls old posters dating back to the Second World War reminded people to *KEEP CALM AND CARRY ON.* The tube station that once would have seen thousands of busy commuters hustling and jostling to get to their destinations was now eerily quiet and deathly still.

Eve stared about her, soaking up the strange atmosphere. She walked quickly to keep up with the others. Tom didn't look too happy, but Clovis was entranced by the whole experience. The only sound that could be heard was the noise of their footsteps, which echoed all about them as they followed Uncle Rufus further down into the station.

'This is really creepy,' said Tom, breaking their silence and looking about him nervously.

'It's only creepy because you are used to underground tube stations being rammed with people,' said Clovis, always the rational one amongst the three friends.

'Yeah, I suppose so,' agreed Eve. 'Come on, Tom, you've got to admit this is kind of cool.'

Suddenly, the tunnel came to an end and Eve, Tom and Clovis found themselves standing at the top of some steps that spiralled tightly down — into what?

'Come on, chaps, don't dawdle.' Uncle Rufus was obviously excited. They looked at each other and began their descent. Round and round the steps went, and they climbed further and further down.

Eventually, to their relief, they stepped out onto a long train platform. The smell of warm, oily air buffeted up the tracks from the long black train tunnel, its open mouth forming a perfect 'O' shape that beckoned ominously to them.

More posters could be seen straight ahead on the opposite wall, advertising everything from soup to new vacuum cleaners. The edge of the platform dropped down into a deep chasm, revealing the silver metal tracks. Eve noticed a tiny mouse scurrying across them, having been rudely disturbed by their arrival.

'Urgh,' she said.

Uncle Rufus began to whistle, which sounded really creepy, as the sound travelled down the tunnel and then immediately came straight back.

'Oh my God! Is someone down there?' whispered Tom.

'No, don't be daft, it's just the professor's echo,' laughed Clovis.

The group followed Uncle Rufus along the deathly quiet platform.

'Where's he taking us?' muttered Tom.

'Not far now,' called back Uncle Rufus, his voice ricocheting down the platform and around the tunnel.

As they came to the end of the long platform, Uncle Rufus took out his torch and shocked everyone by jumping down onto the tracks.

'What the hell?' cried Eve. 'You can't do that, Unc!'

'Don't worry, Eve, it's quite safe,' said Uncle Rufus. He shone his bright torch into the tunnel, trying to show them that it wasn't dangerous. 'There's no electricity down here any more and there haven't been any trains running on this line for years. It's just up ahead, you'll see.'

'Well, this is a very strange place to have your headquarters,' said Eve, following him onto the tracks.

'I know what you mean,' said Clovis. 'I get it has to be kept secret. But this is all a bit extreme.'

'"No trains", he says,' grumbled Tom. He was clearly not happy at being in a dark, damp tunnel. He and Clovis both leaped down, took their phones out and switched on their torches.

Squeak! Squeak!

Everyone froze at the noise.

'It's just a rat.' Uncle Rufus was really laughing now.

Tom had grabbed Eve's arm, not at all happy with the situation. 'I hate rats! Mice . . . I don't like either, but *rats*!' he shouted.

Clovis laughed at him. 'You big baby, Tom,' he said. 'C'mon, he's more scared of you than you are of him.'

Unexpectedly a strong rush of icy wind blew up the tunnel; the noise was quite alarming.

'What the hell was that, Professor?' shouted Tom.

'Don't worry, it's OK.' Uncle Rufus's voice sounded calm, which made Tom and the others feel a bit more comfortable. But they were definitely getting colder.

Eve wished she'd brought her leather biker jacket with her. She held on tight to Tom's arm, all the while wondering where they were going.

Walking carefully down the centre of the tunnel, they kept the tracks on either side of them. The torchlight made their shadows look like huge monsters with elongated arms and legs. Uncle Rufus was a few steps ahead and had begun to whistle once more, until he was interrupted by another eerie noise.

The sound suddenly echoed around them. But this was no rat, echo, blast of air or whistle: it sounded like footsteps. It was definitely somebody walking up behind them.

Everyone stopped moving and turned around. Clovis swiped his torch quickly across the sooty, dirty walls; creating more spooky elongated shadows.

Clovis, Tom and Eve could see a round circle of light from the platform they had just left behind. Clovis then flipped his light back to where the professor was standing in front of them only a few feet away. He wasn't walking. So, who was?

'Professor, did you hear that?' asked Clovis.

'Yes, it's all right, stop worrying, chaps. I think . . . you'll like this.'

The footsteps became louder and louder, then, emerging from the darkness behind Eve, Clovis and Tom, came the outline of a person. It walked towards them with purpose. Slowly the image became clearer, it was slightly see-through and translucent and yet with every step it took, the figure seemed to get brighter. Soon the friends could see it was a man. He wore a very smart suit and on top of his head sat a black bowler hat. His face beamed at the shocked group. In one hand he carried a black umbrella and in the other a briefcase.

Tom, Eve and Clovis just stared, flabbergasted at the sight coming towards them. This very smartly dressed man, walking nonchalantly in the middle of the train tracks, was clearly, and most alarmingly, a ghost!

The spectre had illuminated the whole tunnel. It was as if they had all walked out into a bright sunny day. Everyone held up their hands to shield their eyes, watching, not daring to move.

Tom held his breath, Eve squealed very quietly, '*Oh my God!*' The three friends held on tightly to each other, not quite believing what they were seeing.

As the ghost walked past them all, he turned his head to the three friends and tipped his bowler hat. 'Good morning,' he said gently.

Uncle Rufus let out a loud belly laugh and welcomed the peculiar apparition. 'Well, hello, Percival, what a treat, how are you today?'

'Professor! How lovely to see you. I'm really rather grand. All clear ahead. They're expecting you.' Percival placed his bowler hat back on top of his head and proceeded to walk on, leaving in his wake another blast of fresh, icy air that rushed through them.

Tom, Clovis and Eve stood and stared as they watched the ghost slowly disappear, taking the bright light with him.

'Did we just see that?' whispered Eve.

'Yep,' said Clovis.

'Bloody hell! That was insane!' cried Tom, not quite

believing what he had just witnessed. 'My hands are literally shaking.'

'That was Percival, apparently,' added Eve, shrugging her shoulders as if it were the norm.

Uncle Rufus was now walking further into the tunnel but instantly stopped in his tracks as Eve called out to him.

'Err, Uncle, are you going to, you know, explain about what just happened?'

Uncle Rufus walked back towards them. His torchlight bounced around on the blackened walls.

'Oh, that was Percival, he's a guardian.'

'A guardian?' asked Clovis, looking thrilled.

'Yes, they protect SPI. There are lots of them actually. Some you can't see, but others like Percival are happy for you to see them. Nice chap.' Uncle Rufus ran a hand through his floppy brown hair and sniffed. 'We've been watched from the moment we entered this place. No one gets in or out without the guardians knowing about it. Shall we continue?' he asked, smiling.

'Lead the way, Unc,' said Eve, who wasn't sure what to make of this whole underground adventure.

For years Uncle Rufus had been inventing machines to try to communicate with the dead, she knew that much. And he'd clearly been successful and had helped the inspector in the past. She knew that too. But this place down here, in an old tube station, was bizarre. Watching him talk to a ghost as if it were the most normal thing in the world was really quite astonishing. Eve had thought the professor had told her everything there was to know about his dealings with the paranormal. But just how many more secrets did he have?

After another five minutes of walking, Uncle Rufus suddenly stopped. On the right-hand side of the wall was a door. It was black and wooden and above it was a sign which read in bright red letters *DO NOT ENTER.*

CHAPTER 5

A Welcome to the Society and a Stamp of Approval for Eve

'Right, here we are,' said Uncle Rufus, producing a small, rather detailed key from his trouser pocket. Eve noticed in the torchlight that the key looked familiar. The emblem on the top, she realised, was the same as the insignia on the back of the EVP watches he had made for their first investigation with him — a snake in the shape of a figure of eight eating its own tail. Her uncle had told them that the symbol meant 'life everlasting'. Eve had just assumed that he had designed the symbol himself and that it was special to him. She wondered now if the snake was the emblem for the SPI?

Uncle Rufus put the key into the lock and opened the door. One after the other they stepped through into a dark space. Suddenly, a single lightbulb which dangled from the ceiling flickered into life, bringing a dim, sickly glow into the room. There were knobs and dials embedded into a white console which ran along the side of the wall. At the end of the room, facing them, was a pair of plain doors with a button set into the wall on the side.

'Is it an elevator?' asked Eve.

'Oh no, not another one!' moaned Tom. 'Last time we got into one of these, we ended up in a ghost-infested Second World War bunker.' He shivered at the memory of their last adventure.

'It's all OK,' laughed Uncle Rufus, pressing the lift's call button. 'We're going somewhere nice and bright this time.'

Instantly the two doors swooshed open to reveal an everyday-looking elevator.

'Everyone in,' said Uncle Rufus, standing at the side and waving the three friends in enthusiastically. Everybody walked into the little white rectangular box and as soon as the doors whipped closed, corny lift music began to pipe through the tinny speakers on the walls.

The elevator rumbled into action: the noise was quite disconcerting, its creaking and moaning reminded Clovis of his grandma getting up from a chair.

'Are you sure this is safe?' asked Tom, looking a little worried.

'It's fine,' reassured Uncle Rufus.

'Are we going up or down? I can't tell,' said Clovis. He placed his large hands on the walls of the elevator. 'How odd,' he whispered to himself.

'No one knows,' said Uncle Rufus cryptically.

'Hang on,' said Eve. 'So, you don't know whether we are going up or down?' She didn't look happy, which made Uncle Rufus laugh out loud. 'Where on earth is this place?' she asked.

Suddenly the lift began to shudder, causing Eve to cry out in alarm. She flung her arms out, making a grab for her uncle then suddenly, much to her relief, the elevator came to an abrupt stop. It dinged loudly to let its riders know that they had arrived at their destination and the doors instantly whooshed open. Uncle Rufus straightened his tie, smoothed down his hair under his hat and walked out. The others cautiously stepped into a vast white room that seemed to be totally lined with marble.

'Wow! What is this place?' Tom spun around in the immense room. His words echoed back. 'Are we in heaven?'

'All will be explained in a little while,' whispered Uncle Rufus. 'Let's go and see the inspector, she'll be the one who gives you all the answers.' Uncle Rufus gently pushed Eve forward, steering her and her friends to a desk that was positioned in the centre of the room. It too was made out of marble and sitting behind it was a very beautiful young woman. She wore a smart blue jacket, white shirt and blue tie. Her hair was silver and coiled around the top of her head.

'Good afternoon, Professor,' her voice tinkled softly, and as she smiled Eve swore she saw a twinkling light sparkle from her perfect teeth.

'Wow!' whispered Clovis.

Eve nudged him in the ribs. 'Close your mouth, Clovis.' She placed a finger under his jaw, closing it with a snap.

'Well, hello, Celeste.' Uncle Rufus shuffled nervously from

one foot to the other, his voice a little deeper than usual. 'Lovely to see you again,' he crooned.

Eve was stunned, she had never seen her uncle act this way with a woman before. She peered closer at him and noticed his cheeks were well and truly flushed.

'He fancies her,' whispered Tom.

'Shut up, you.' Eve elbowed Tom in the ribs.

Her uncle turned to see what the yelp was, but all he saw was Eve and Tom smiling sweetly at him. Uncle Rufus turned back round and continued to make pleasantries with Celeste. Finally, he introduced the others, and she greeted them all kindly and invited them to check in.

Everyone watched as Uncle Rufus made his way into what appeared to be a photo booth. He smiled and pulled the blue curtain across.

The others said nothing but watched as a blinding white light blasted from underneath the curtain. He came out looking a little dazed.

'Eve, it's your turn,' tinkled Celeste.

Eve stepped forward and looked back at her uncle, not sure what to expect.

'It's quite all right, Eve, it's just to make sure we are who we say we are.' Uncle Rufus nodded approvingly.

Eve went behind the curtain. In front of her was a stool which she nervously sat on. A dark glass screen was positioned in front of her, instructing Eve to place her fingers in some ominous-looking silver tubes which sat on the top of a small counter in front. She breathed out loudly, shaking her head at the madness of it all. Placing her fingers gingerly into the cold metal tubes. Suddenly a loud click, a whirr, a bang and a chopping noise exploded from behind the glass, followed by a blinding light. For a split-second Eve could just make out a swirl of colours around her reflection, and then the light was abruptly extinguished, plunging Eve into total darkness. Next the screen typed out a message, 'Thank you, Eve Proud, have a wonderful day!'

Clovis and Tom took their turns next and both boys came out of the photo booth looking a little disorientated.

'See, nothing to it,' said Uncle Rufus.

'What is that thing?' asked Tom, still looking rather dishevelled.

'It takes pictures of people's auras,' explained Uncle Rufus. 'Everyone has one and everyone's is different. It's a bit like having your fingerprints taken but this is an impression of your soul and the energies that surround you. No two are the same. It's very intricate, and an aura picture is impossible to fake.'

'No way! Do we get to see the pictures?' asked Clovis excitedly. 'I'd love to see what our auras look like.'

Celeste smiled beautifully and explained politely that unfortunately no one could see the pictures but that everyone who entered the main doors had to have their soul credentials and their auras checked. 'It's the law. Now you're all in our database,' she giggled lightly. Tom giggled back.

'Oh my God! Tom! Control yourself,' whispered Eve through gritted teeth. She was beginning to find Celeste a little nauseating.

'Detective Inspector Rutherford is expecting you, if you would like to go through.' Celeste gestured at a large set of doors behind her. Inscribed into each door was the insignia of the self-eating snake.

'Life everlasting,' muttered Eve. The doors swung open seemingly on their own to reveal an enormous room filled with row upon row of desks where many people were working away, tapping on computer keyboards or talking on phones. At the very back of the room, a library of old books lined the whole length of the wall and to the far right-hand side of it there was a spiral staircase that seemed to go up for ever.

'That's a brilliant painting of the night sky. It's so real,' gasped Eve, turning around to take in the full view of what she thought was the ceiling.

'That's not a painting, my dear girl. That *is* the sky, in fact, that is the universe. You will never see anything quite like it anywhere else.' Uncle Rufus was also looking skywards.

'It's a bit like yours, Uncle,' said Eve.

'Yes, it is but this is the *real* thing, Eve,' said Uncle Rufus.

'But I don't understand. It's light outside, the middle of the day. So how come the sky here is dark and so, so bright? I mean wow! Look!' Clovis pointed at one of the brightest shooting stars he had ever seen.

'What you are looking at is called "the Veil", but more of

that later. Come on,' said Uncle Rufus. 'I can see the inspector over there.'

Everyone followed Uncle Rufus's gaze and noticed that standing on the spiral staircase was a figure with a mop of grey curly hair.

'Yoohoo! I say! I'm up here.' The figure waved, much to everyone's amusement.

Uncle Rufus led the way down the central aisle of the vast room. It was quite noisy, people talking on headsets, tapping away on their computers. It looked and sounded like an ordinary office but as they walked by the desks, they caught snippets of strange conversations.

'So, is the poltergeist throwing things now?' asked a young woman in a slow American drawl, as she briskly filed her long fingernails, chewed gum and swung her swivel chair from side to side.

'An exorcism? I'll put you through,' said a rather thin, pointy gentleman. He looked up at the new visitors and in surprise raised a pair of very hairy eyebrows.

'I'm sorry but for that particular haunting you'll need to speak to one of our Roman historians,' said an older lady. She wore a long, brightly coloured silk scarf, and a crystal ring on every finger. She punched one of the many buttons on her phone's console, sighed heavily then sat back, smiling warmly at Uncle Rufus and the others as they walked by.

'This is so weird,' said Tom quietly out of the corner of his mouth.

'Shush,' replied Clovis, who was trying to listen into a very exciting conversation about a science department.

None of the workers seemed bothered or disturbed by their presence. Eve stopped in her tracks as she came across one desk whose occupant didn't seem to be there at all and yet *something* seemed to be. Clovis and Tom had spotted the same thing and all three watched in amazement as a rubber stamp moved all on its own, stamping out a symbol that they had come to recognise onto lots of white envelopes.

'Are you seeing this?' asked Clovis. His eyes bulged like huge saucers, not quite believing what he was witnessing. 'What the hell *is* this place?' he whispered, more to himself than to the others.

Tom and Eve nodded, never taking their eye off the rubber stamp, which seemed to be picking up speed.

'Is a *ghost* doing that?' asked Eve. She scrunched up her eyes and pressed her face closer to the desk and the self-moving rubber stamp. What happened next came as a shock. Suddenly the rubber stamp smacked Eve right on the cheek. She screeched out loud then held her face.

'Oh, my dear girl, are you all right?' asked Uncle Rufus, rushing back to see what had happened.

Eve slowly removed her hand from her face, revealing an image of the self-eating snake which was now well and truly emblazoned upon her face. Eve turned to Tom, Clovis and Uncle Rufus and was met with an explosion of laughter.

'What?' she sizzled, eyes wide and startled.

'It's your face,' snorted Clovis. 'Seems you're property of the SPI.'

'Look!' said Tom, holding up his phone so Eve could look at her reflection. Sure enough, there for all to see was a large black self-eating snake printed onto her cheek. She tried to rub it off but nothing happened.

'It will come off, Eve, don't worry,' Uncle Rufus assured her.

'Who put it there?' asked Eve through gritted teeth.

'Oh, that will be Cedric. He's a poltergeist, and a very playful one at that.' Everyone turned round to find Detective Inspector Rutherford standing directly behind them.

CHAPTER 6

Explanations and Revelations

Even though small in stature, Inspector Rutherford radiated a certain strength, something formidable that neither Tom, Clovis nor Eve could put into words. Her head was held high and proud, her hands clasped behind her back.

'Well now,' she said, bringing her hands together and clapping with excitement. 'I'm so pleased you're here. Journey all right?'

'It wasn't what we were expecting,' answered Eve honestly.

'Aha, met Percival, did we?' laughed the inspector. 'Oh, and Cedric,' she said, noticing the stamp on Eve's face. 'Here,' and she offered her a wet wipe.

Then she clicked her tongue and swung her glass beaded necklace from side to side. 'Oh, I'm so pleased you're here,' she said, stepping back and admiring the small group of friends standing in front of her. 'I've so much to show you and, of course, explain. Shall we go upstairs to my office? Cedric, will you be so kind as to ask Celeste to bring some refreshments up? There's a dear.'

The inspector looked to the space at the desk where the

rogue rubber stamp had attacked Eve. Everyone watched in amazement as the chair flew backwards. The desk thumped loudly, sending paperclips of every colour flying into the air and heavy, stomping footsteps could be heard walking off, presumably to the beautiful and angelic Celeste.

'He's bit bad-tempered, but our Cedric is a good soul and incredibly reliable when needed. Now, come, come, my dears,' barked the inspector over her shoulder as she began to walk up the spiral staircase.

Everyone followed and it wasn't long before puffing and panting could be heard.

'How high does this go?' complained Tom.

'Ha, ha, Tom, not far now — *you're* supposed to be the sportsman.' The inspector guffawed at her own little joke.

Up and up, they climbed, turning continuously in a tight circle. Just as Eve thought she was going to have to stop because of the dizziness and breathlessness, they arrived at the top.

A cosy room awaited them, a stark contrast to the brightness of the rooms below. Dark wooden panelling hugged the walls, and paintings of very stern, fusty old men and women looked down their unimpressed noses at the new arrivals. A welcoming fire crackled in a small fireplace. Books lined the walls, a plain wooden desk faced them, and a large globe on a stand was positioned in the corner.

'Well, here we all are,' said the inspector, settling herself behind her desk. 'Please do take a seat,' she instructed.

Eve, Tom and Clovis sat on the leather sofa in front of the inspector's desk. Uncle Rufus plonked himself down in a rather oversized, comfortable-looking armchair.

A faint knock came from the door.

'Come in,' the inspector called, reminding Tom of his old headteacher.

The door opened and in walked Celeste, carrying a tray piled high with tea and cakes. She seemed to glide across the floor, not a hair out of place.

'Oh, thank you, Celeste. Can you make sure I'm not disturbed while our guests are here?'

Celeste smiled, nodded her perfect coiffed head and glided once more out of the room. Uncle Rufus, Clovis and Tom followed her every move. Eve watched them and snorted with irritation.

Inspector Rutherford poured the hot tea into the cups then passed the cakes around. As Uncle Rufus and the inspector talked, the teenagers' minds were a-whirr with questions. Where were they exactly? Why had they been asked to come? What were all those people doing down there? What was *the Veil*? What was a guardian? Was Celeste an angel? And who the hell was Cedric?

As if the inspector could read their minds, she stood up, took a few sips of tea then placed her cup onto her desk. She looked at the group assembled in front of her and cleared her throat.

'Well now, I know you're wondering why I've asked you all to come here today and you've probably guessed that this is no ordinary police station, correct?' Tom, Eve and Clovis nodded, never taking their eyes off the unusual woman.

'Well, as I understand it, the professor here —' she nodded at Uncle Rufus — 'has already divulged the name of our society to you, and everyone here —' the inspector wafted her hand around the old pictures on the walls as if they were real people — 'was very impressed with your work on the Epping Forest case.' The inspector clacked her glass beads. 'The society has been running for generations and only a handful of trusted people outside of this organisation know of its existence.'

Eve, Tom and Clovis all leaned further forward, keen not to miss a word.

The inspector carried on: 'Its investigators needed protection and help and so seventy years ago, with assistance from a classified department within the government, it became a secret unit within the police force,' she continued. 'It brings together like-minded people who believe in the afterlife and have the ability to communicate with it. We know about hauntings going on all over the country and make sure that the person or persons involved get the very best advice and help. We have lots of investigators who know exactly how to handle every type of haunting, good or bad. We train each and every one and only then after years of study and investigations in the field, do they qualify as SPI members. There are many departments within the organisation, one for historical cases, one for poltergeists, an excellent one for inventions — the professor's favourite, I believe.' She smiled warmly at Uncle Rufus. 'But there are many more. There are experts in every field, covering not just the paranormal but all aspects of the supernatural and of witchcraft. Many countries around the world now have an SPI branch but I'm proud to say that our society in London is the original and the headquarters for the whole organisation. Our main aim is to make sure that every departed soul is cared for and enabled to go on to their rightful place.'

'Rightful place?' asked Eve.

'Yes.' The inspector picked up her tea cup again in one hand and a little cake in the other. 'You see, when we die, most of us go quite happily to our new home, the Otherside. Some souls struggle to get there, mostly because they are afraid or confused and, as you know only too well, this can result in a haunting. Most souls are happy to be shown the way, others, if they have done something bad in this life, will be fearful of what awaits them because they're not allowed into the Otherside. Sadly they dig their heels in. They can become wretched and quite bad-tempered.'

'Do you mean they're frightened to go to Hell?' asked Tom.

'We don't call it Hell,' said Uncle Rufus. 'We prefer to call it the Abyss.'

The word 'Abyss' was whispered, and everyone noticed the inspector shiver as the word was spoken out loud.

She went on. 'Our main job here at SPI is to send all the trapped souls through the right door.'

'Door?' asked Clovis, chomping down on a chocolate biscuit.

'Yes, there are no *doors*, as such, but it's an image we ask the souls to imagine. It's a symbol that we humans can relate to, you know, coming and going, as one door opens, another closes, et cetera, et cetera.' She waved the tea cup back and forth in one hand to emphasise the point, and everyone watched on as it wobbled precariously. In the other hand she held firmly onto the cake, crumbs falling to the floor like a fine shower of rain.

'Do you remember when you saw Finlay Bains go into the light?' said Uncle Rufus.

'How could we forget? It was so peaceful,' whispered Eve, remembering their last adventure. They had found the body of a Second World War soldier and in doing so had helped his soul to move on.

'Well, that's exactly what SPI do. They help souls move on to their new homes,' said Uncle Rufus, looking rather proud.

'So, you're exorcists,' said Clovis.

'To an extent, yes. But we don't just rid people and places of spirits, we facilitate the movement of spirits to a final resting place — be it good or bad.'

'So, you're one of these investigators, Uncle Rufus?'

'I have been, yes. I've done my training. But I've tended

to work more on the inventions to help the investigators,' he said.

'Wow,' said Clovis. This was starting to sound like his dream job. 'OK, so if we accept and believe all that, and it's a lot to process, I still don't understand where we *are* exactly. Are we deep underground? Feels like it, but I can see the stars in the sky, all the constellations. You said, Professor, that what we were looking up at was the universe, but how can that be?' Clovis was clearly struggling with everything that he had witnessed so far. He carried on talking to himself, desperately trying to figure out where they were. It was like a gigantic puzzle to him and he needed to solve it. He scrunched his eyes tight shut and tilted his head back. 'We came through the old tube station and then got into the lift . . . I couldn't work out if we were going up or down.' He moved his fingers about in the air as if following an invisible map.

'We went backwards,' said Eve, nudging Clovis.

'It felt like we went to the side to me. Really odd,' mumbled Tom.

The inspector put her tea cup down on to her desk and brushed the crumbs off her jacket. Then she put her hands behind her back and began to pace back and forth. 'Clovis, Eve, Tom, I realise this is all a little daunting for you, but I hope my explanations will help a little.' She stopped pacing and turned swiftly towards her audience, making her glass beads swing out in an impressive twinkling arc. 'We are located in a place called the Veil. Well, the entrance chamber of the Veil, if you will. When you first walked in, you would have noticed the beautiful night sky above you. It's no ordinary sky, it is the thin barrier between our world and the Otherside. I think you now know that the Otherside is the place most of us travel to when we leave this life. Are you with me so far?'

She stopped pacing and looked to Tom, Eve and Clovis. They all nodded again in unison.

'Good . . . the Veil is extremely precious and delicate, it's a fine layer of space that separates our two planes. It's normally the first place you come to when you die. There are many doors or gateways that open to allow souls through into it. So, for instance any loved ones that you may have lost would have been brought through a door into the Veil, where they would have been met by a family member or their life guide. Once they have grown accustomed to the fact that they have left their old life behind, and it's time to begin their next life, they are then taken to the Otherside, to live on in paradise. So, you see —' the inspector waved her hands about and tipped her head back, as if talking to some invisible person above her —'it's a very special place, and one that must be monitored at all times. SPI have many guardians who protect the Veil. They protect us and everything we do in facilitating the dead in their journeys. I know you met Percival on the way here, he's one of our finest.'

'So, it's kind of like a waiting room?' asked Eve, her eyes wide with excitement.

'Yes,' laughed the inspector. 'But a very nice one. Are you with me so far?'

'I think so,' said Tom. 'So what are *we* doing here? Just checking, we're not dead, are we?'

'That's a good question, Tom. But no, you're not dead,' the inspector chuckled. 'Far from it. You're very much alive. The SPI is protected, it's a safe place for us mere mortals.'

The inspector walked over to one of the pictures on the wall: it was of a rather gruff-looking gentleman with an enormous white beard. She looked at it and smiled affectionately. 'This is my father, Joshua Rutherford, a fine man. He introduced me to SPI when I was sixteen. I know it's hard to imagine me as anything but old, eh?' Detective Inspector Rutherford began to laugh, and the others smiled because she was right, somehow: they couldn't picture this wonderful, eccentric woman ever being young like them.

The inspector continued, 'Well, it came to me recently, after the incident at Epping Forest really, that we don't have enough young people in the organisation any more. You're only a few years younger than I was when I joined. I know the professor has been giving you some informal training, and Clovis and Eve, you each seem to be particularly passionate about the paranormal. He's been keeping me informed of all your progress and now, after a meeting with members of the board, we'd like to make your training more official. To send you on assignments and train you to be fully-fledged investigators. If that's what you'd like.'

'Yes, please!' squealed Eve, jumping up quickly with excitement. 'Oh my gosh! Yes, yes, yes!'

'That would be amazing,' added Clovis, standing up too. Eve's excitement was contagious. 'Would I be able to get involved a bit with inventions as well, do you think?'

Uncle Rufus and the inspector nodded. Clovis placed an arm round Eve's shoulders and smiled broadly, his mind a-buzz, thinking what the science department would be like.

'And what about you, Tom?' asked Detective Inspector Rutherford.

'Don't get me wrong . . .' said Tom, looking a little uncomfortable. He dropped his head and began to pick at some dry skin on his thumb, his hair flopping forward and shielding his face from everyone. 'I'd love to get involved, but you're right, I'm not sure I'm cut out for this like the others are. I'm not as brave as Eve and I'm not as clever as Clovis. I don't know what my mum and dad would make of it either. My dad's not the most easy-going, you see, and my mum, well, she's out of town at the moment.' Tom's face crumpled and Eve leaned down to squeeze his arm. 'I'm just not sure it's a good time for me right now.'

'There are many different personalities on the team,' said the inspector, 'and I think you'll make a fine investigator. But if this *isn't* for you, I respect that.'

'No, Tom,' said Eve. She sat back down beside her best friend and wrapped her arms around his waist. 'You've got to be a part of it. We do everything together.'

'I just . . .'

'You don't have to decide now,' said the inspector. 'Sleep on it. Or maybe go along on the first mission I'm proposing and see how you feel.'

'Do we have to do special training? You said that all investigators have to go through years of training,' said Tom, looking a little worried.

'Maybe in time, but you've been learning alongside one of the best instructors we have already. The professor will continue to teach and guide you, but this time on real missions. You have already shown so much potential, and we believe here at SPI that in time you will each become great investigators. All of you,' she said pointedly, looking at Tom.

Tom and Eve stood up, grabbed Clovis to them and beamed at each other excitedly. In that moment they all understood that they were about to start a whole new chapter in their lives. Just to know that they would have the opportunity to work together, and have adventures that none of their other friends could ever dream of, was amazing.

'That's settled, then,' said Detective Inspector Rutherford.

'Well, yes, Ruthers, but I *would* like to know what the case is before I agree to involve the youngsters,' said Uncle Rufus.

'Absolutely,' said the inspector. 'I know you are keen to protect the children, as are we, but I think this first case will interest you, Rufus, and also be ideal for our new recruits.'

She opened a large, ancient-looking book on her desk at its centre and then seemed to press something inside it. Suddenly the panelled wall on the left-hand side of the room began to slide up to reveal several large television monitors. On one screen a graphic of a compass spun around slowly over the top of an image of the globe. The other screens showed iconic locations from around the world. Big Ben in London, the Sydney Opera House in Australia, the Statue of Liberty in New York, the Colosseum in Rome, the Eiffel Tower in Paris. Plus some others that Tom and Eve didn't recognise. A smaller screen displayed a series of columns and numbers. All were in different colours, some moving up and down, some quicker than others. They fluctuated constantly.

'Wow!' whispered Clovis, stepping towards the monitors. His mouth was open in amazement and he tripped over his own size-eleven feet to get a closer look.

Detective Inspector Rutherford stepped protectively in front of the screens and began to explain what they were used for. 'We like to keep an eye on as many countries as we can. So, the numbers you see going up and down represent souls moving into different realms. The numbers in red are souls that refuse to move on. They're haunting buildings, making a nuisance of themselves, and that's where *we* come in. Each country has their own society, and we keep in constant contact with each other throughout the day. We all deal with our own vicinity, unless there is some sort of crisis, and then of course everyone comes together to help.

Troublesome or confused souls can cause untold damage and distress, and I know you've all had experience of this yourselves. And because of that experience and the way in which you handled yourselves during the Epping Forest investigation, we'd be honoured if you started on this new case that's just come in. You are perfect for it. Of course, you will have the professor with you at all times.'

'OK, so what's the case?' asked Uncle Rufus, taking out a notebook and small pencil from his top pocket. Clovis followed suit, opening a notes app on his phone.

Eve and Tom did nothing, knowing their friend would take everything down and more. He had probably been recording the whole conversation anyhow. Clovis knew full well that his notes would be pored over later by a very grateful Eve and Tom. He didn't mind.

The inspector tapped on the screen, showing Big Ben in London from above, and immediately the camera zoomed out to show a satellite image of the whole city. Then Inspector Rutherford double tapped on the screen and the camera zoomed in closer and closer on another part of the city.

'I recognise that place, look!' blurted out Eve excitedly. 'It's Whitechapel! We live near there.' She had muscled her way closer to the screen, her nose practically touching the glass.

Again, the inspector moved the camera in a different direction, along the streets of Whitechapel, until the picture froze on the rooftop of a school building.

The inspector cleared her throat, took a deep breath and began: 'What I'm about to tell you is top secret and you must *never* talk about it to anyone outside of this society. Do you understand? In fact . . .' Her voice dropped and a steely look bored into them all. 'In fact, the SPI must *never* be mentioned to anyone who is not a member. If it is, the person found responsible will be dealt with.'

She began to pace about back and forth again, and the children nodded gravely as one.

She went on. 'Have you all heard of Jack the Ripper?'

Eve, Clovis and Tom looked at each other in confusion.

'The Victorian serial killer?' said Clovis.

'That's right,' said the inspector. 'Well, his ghost . . . it's back.'

CHAPTER 7

The Ghost of a Victorian Serial Killer and a Hunch

Uncle Rufus was clearly shocked at the news and sat down slowly.

'I'm sorry,' said Eve, looking confused. 'What do you mean *it's back*? Are you saying that his ghost has been seen before?'

Detective Inspector Rutherford tapped the large screen on the wall and instantly a black and white image of a man came into view. It wasn't very clear; the picture had obviously been taken by a CCTV camera. It was odd, the streets looked modern, but the man was dressed in old-fashioned Victorian clothing. He wore a long cloak and black top hat. In his gloved hand he carried a doctor's bag. His face wasn't very clear, as his head was cocked slightly to one side, the brim of his hat tipping over to conceal half of his face.

Eve stared at the screen and the image and, as if in a trance, she put her hand out and traced the lines of the ghostly figure with her fingers.

'There's something about him I recognise,' she said, looking intently at the picture of the man.

'What you're looking at is, we believe, the ghost of the infamous Jack the Ripper.' The inspector whispered the statement as if she were frightened that the ghost himself would hear her.

Immediately Eve snatched her fingers away as if she had been scalded.

'I presume you all know of this man's crimes?' asked the inspector, tapping the image on the screen.

'He's one of, if not *the* most infamous serial killer in world history,' replied Clovis, pushing his large, black-rimmed glasses up the bridge of his nose. He then took a deep breath, ready to reel off a list of facts.

'You asked for it,' whispered Tom, rolling his eyes at Eve. She snorted with a laugh.

'Jack became famous not only for his shocking killings of five women in Whitechapel in the eighteen-eighties, but also because his identity has never been discovered. Many people believe he may have killed more than just the five women, but no one has ever found conclusive evidence. He also liked to plague the police and the press by sending them letters. He began some of the letters with "Dear Boss" and signed them as Jack the Ripper. His murders caused panic and fear throughout London. The government was so desperate to capture him that the police questioned numerous suspects, from a local butcher, a barber, a bootmaker, and a morgue assistant, to Queen Victoria's grandson Albert, I believe.'

Clovis stopped talking, took a long breath and looked

about him. Everyone stared. He was used to this reaction. He seemed to be able to remember things so precisely. Sometimes he scared himself at just how much information he was able to keep in his head.

'Well, young man, that was impressive,' sighed the inspector. 'I can see why the professor speaks so highly of you.'

Clovis looked out of the corner of his eye at Tom and Eve, worried that he might have annoyed them. Sometimes he knew he could go too far. He couldn't help it, he just *needed* to share information. To his relief, they were smiling, clearly proud of him.

He looked back at the image on the screen. 'How come you know that is definitely him?' he asked. 'I mean, since we know the question of his identity has confounded the police and experts to this day.'

'We know it's him because . . . I've spoken to him.' The inspector went to her desk, pulled out her huge leather chair and sat down. 'As well as being in the SPI I also trained in normal police duties. It was a very busy time as I had lots of paranormal cases to deal with but also earthly cases to solve. I first came across the ghost of Jack the Ripper when a cold case landed on my desk at Scotland Yard. A woman's body had been unearthed by some builders. They had been drilling into a concrete floor in an old warehouse and discovered her skeletal remains. After the pathologist had dated the bones, we discovered she had been killed in the most brutal way. The skeleton dated back to the late eighteen hundreds, and the marks on her bones led us to believe she had been murdered in a similar manner to that of Jack's other victims. We couldn't identify her but that night when I went home and to bed, the nightmares began. Jack came to me in a truly horrific dream and told me that he had done it. In fact, he told me he had committed many more murders that the police would never know about. It was so real, so terrifying. It affected me for a very long time. His face was never clear to me, but he kept showing me all the murders he had committed over and over again. I checked and cross-checked all the details he had shown me with the archive files at Scotland Yard and they all matched up. But then he started showing me crimes he planned to commit in the future. They were so clear. One dream showed a poor young policeman on my team lying deathly still, covered in blood in a dark alleyway.'

The others watched as the inspector took a glass and began to fill it with water from a jug. Her hand shook slightly as she carried on telling her bizarre story.

'I began to research the old cases from scratch. I became obsessed with him. Every spare moment I had, I gave to the investigation of Jack the Ripper. I knew there was more to my dreams than I understood. I tried to contact Jack with the help of the SPI but we just couldn't get to him. He was proving to be the most elusive ghost we had ever come across and the most dangerous. I was aware that certain negative spirits can harm humans and I was worried Jack's ghost might be one of those. Then one night my worst fears came true.

I was called out to a small alleyway in Whitechapel. One of our young officers had been viciously attacked in the exact same way Jack had shown me in my dream. A nightmare, to be more precise. I'll never unsee the images of the officer's body. It had been dissected like an animal in exactly the way he had shown me in the dream. Even down to the exact placement of each body part on the floor. I was shocked and horrified. I knew Jack had committed this heinous crime and that he was goading me.'

Detective Inspector Rutherford took a sip of water, closed her eyes briefly as if in pain. The others looked to each other, wide-eyed, intrigued and yet frightened. They could see that this ghost had really traumatised the inspector.

She opened her eyes and expelled a long breath. The others could tell she was trying to get the images of the young officer's body out of her mind. She physically shook her head and then looked up to the ceiling. After a short and awkward silence, the inspector continued with her story. Her voice was a whisper; Clovis leaned forward so he could hear her a little clearer.

'It was in that moment, standing in the alleyway, that I knew we had to stop him. I had to track down his ghost and do it quickly. I needed something special and so that's when I went to Rufus. I knew he was a gifted investigator but when I saw his work and his machines, I was awestruck and fascinated. So, Rufus, myself and another talented investigator, Mr Sa—'

At that moment, Uncle Rufus interrupted the inspector with a loud cough. Eve and the others noticed the strange look that passed between them.

'Oh,' said Eve. 'Who was this other investigator?'

'No one, Eve,' replied the inspector briskly, looking down at her shiny brown shoes.

'He's no longer with SPI, so it doesn't matter,' said Uncle Rufus, looking rather uncomfortable.

Detective Inspector Rutherford seemed to shake the negative memories from her head, then looked up at her guests before carrying on with her story. 'And so began the long quest to find and bring down the ghost of Jack the Ripper. I'm glad to say we did eventually capture and bind him to the confines of an unmarked grave, but somehow he's managed to escape.'

'So you must have discovered his true identity then?' said Clovis, looking like he was about to burst with excitement.

'Good question, young man, but no, we didn't. All I can say is that he is evil in its purest form.'

'What I want to know, is *how* he escaped the binding incantation?' said Uncle Rufus.

Eve looked to her uncle and noticed he seemed agitated and nervous.

The inspector took another sip of water. 'I don't know, Rufus, but one thing I'm certain of is that he's back. Yesterday, we received a report from the deputy head at Whitechapel Primary School. He claims that one of his teachers reported seeing a terrifying apparition, which he dismissed at the time but he himself has now seen the ghosts of two Victorian children and a ghostly apparition fitting the description of our chap here.' The inspector nodded at the shadowed face on the screen. 'The deputy head was in a bad state, bruised, badly shocked and . . . *burned*. After refusing to talk to anyone, eventually I managed to get him to confide in me. When he told his story and described the ghost to me, I knew with a heavy heart that for some inexplicable reason, the ghost of Jack the Ripper had come back. I didn't think it was possible for his ghost to rise up once more, but obviously I was wrong. And for some reason he is haunting a primary school, of all places. He's already hurt an adult — imagine what he might do to children when they return after their holidays. We must do everything we can to stop him and this time send him away for eternity.'

'It's him!' shouted Eve suddenly. She stepped back from the screen, her hand over her mouth in shock.

Uncle Rufus rushed to her. 'Eve . . . are you all right?'

'It's him! Don't you recognise him, Tom? Clovis?'

'No,' said Tom, shaking his head. Moving closer, he squinted, trying to see if he could identify the black shadowy figure on the screen.

'He does look familiar, now you mention it,' said Clovis. He took his black-rimmed glasses off, wiped them on his T-shirt, then put them back on and leaned in further for a better look.

'Don't you remember last year? We were on our bikes and took the shortcut through the cemetery.'

'Oh my God!' whispered Tom. The penny had dropped. 'You're right, we *have* seen him. It's the guy who jumped out at us and scared us to death.'

'I remember now, I thought it was a man in fancy dress, but it wasn't, was it?' said Clovis, looking concerned.

'It was him. It was the ghost of Jack the Ripper,' whimpered Eve.

'Which cemetery was this?' asked the inspector with urgency.

'Highgate. We had been to the shopping centre at Brent Cross and decided to cut through the cemetery. We got the fright of our lives.'

'Yeah,' added Tom. 'It was the night before Halloween, loads of people were out that week trick-or-treating wearing costumes, so we just assumed . . .'

Eve shuddered and rubbed her arms. 'It was his eyes, they were red. I've never forgotten that. I was sure it was a ghost but the next day we convinced ourselves that it wasn't and that Clovis was right and it was just a man playing a Halloween prank.'

'But it *was* a ghost and now we know *who* it was,' said Tom, chewing on his thumbnail.

Eve, Tom and Clovis all noticed the look that the inspector gave Uncle Rufus. A secret, knowing look.

'Highgate Cemetery,' said Inspector Rutherford, 'is the

place where we managed to contain his spirit. We even placed a cross in an unmarked grave so he would remain there for eternity. A binding spell was the only thing that seemed to work on his spirit. Somehow he has obviously freed himself.'

'But how?' asked Uncle Rufus, looking confused.

'That, my dear friend, we may never know. But what I need right now are some answers. I need you all to go to the school tomorrow and find out as much as you can about what happened to the deputy head.'

'I'm not being rude,' said Tom, 'but why are you sending us? This sounds like a pretty serious case.'

'Oh, it is,' said Inspector Rutherford. 'But don't worry, it's not the Ripper we want *you* to deal with. It's those children. Spirits of children are often very wary and frightened of adults. I think you three will be perfect to help them. I need you to find out who they are and why they are haunting with Jack. Are they connected to the school in any way? Or are they connected to him? I want them taken to the Otherside, and then we can deal with Jack. I believe the professor here will guide you through that one. But, and this is a big but, you *must* leave the ghost of Jack to the professor.'

Everyone nodded.

'Good. Professor, the deputy head of the school, Mr Wilson, will be expecting your call. You know where I am if you need me.'

CHAPTER 8

A Street with Two Names

The group of newly appointed investigators made their way back out of the SPI. They walked through the tunnels of the old underground station, and, after climbing back up the gruelling heights of spiral steps, eventually emerged into the normality of the London streets. As they walked along, they talked constantly in excited chatter, mindful not to mention the SPI or the case they had just been given.

On the top deck of the empty bus, Uncle Rufus sat behind the three friends, frantically scribbling down notes, his eyes glazed over as if in some far distant land.

Tom, Eve and Clovis huddled together and whispered amongst themselves. Even though they were aware that they were the only ones on the top deck of the bus, they knew they couldn't be too careful who could hear them and only spoke vaguely about their next ghost hunt and what it would be like.

Finally, when the bus reached their stop, they jumped off and made their way quickly to Eve's house. After being greeted by a very excited Mr Pig and a burping, snuffling

Boris, Uncle Rufus got straight to it and made a phone call to Mr Wilson. The others busied themselves, putting coats and shoes away. Clovis popped the kettle on and Tom began to feed the toaster with bread. All the while they kept an ear open, listening in to Uncle Rufus's conversation on the phone in the hallway.

'I'm so sorry to hear that, Mr Wilson, but I'm pleased to know that you're on the mend. So, you said there were two children? Yes . . . dripping in water. Did they say anything to you? No . . . Were there any historical deaths at the school or indeed on the land, Mr Wilson? No . . . Oh, I see. And you say a man appeared too . . . ? Yes . . . Could you describe him for me? . . . I see . . . Do you think we could come to the school, Mr Wilson? It would be most beneficial for us if you could show us exactly where you encountered the activity.'

Eve, Tom and Clovis stopped what they were doing and began to edge closer to the hallway.

'Perfect! Tomorrow morning, then. Can I just check the address? Yes, Henriques Street, Whitechapel. Got it, we'll be there. Thank you, goodbye, Mr Wilson.'

Uncle Rufus put the phone down and ran his fingers through his hair. He blew out a long breath and shook his head.

'Well?' asked Eve.

'Poor chap,' answered her uncle. 'He really has had a hard time. I could still hear his voice shaking. Whatever he experienced nearly gave him a heart attack.'

'What exactly did he see, Professor?' asked Tom nervously. He was feeling anxious about this ghost and was more than happy to let the professor deal with him. And the ghostly children upset him. He wondered to himself why two children would be haunting a school? He thought how lonely they must be feeling.

'What Mr Wilson saw,' continued Uncle Rufus, walking into the kitchen, 'sounds terrifying. In fact, after speaking to him, I'm not sure this *is* the right first SPI case for you all to be investigating. It might be too much.'

He began to butter the toast a little too vigorously. Eve watched her uncle carefully, he was agitated again.

'No, Uncle, this is perfect for us.' She placed her hand on his shoulder. 'The inspector thinks we'll be all right. She said herself that the children need young people to help them.'

Uncle Rufus put the butter knife down and turned to his niece, his face full of concern.

'I know what the inspector said . . . it's just this Jack the Ripper ghost, well . . . I've come across him before.'

'Yes, we know, Uncle. You put him in a binding spell with Rutherford.'

'Eventually, yes, but I'd encountered him before that.'

Uncle Rufus took the mug of tea that Clovis offered him and all eyes were firmly fixed on the professor as he sat down at the kitchen table.

'It was at the beginning, when I had just joined the SPI.

Ruthers put me on the case with another investigator called Anwaar Saygh to begin with.'

'Anwaar?' said Eve.

'It's Arabic, it means "light",' replied Clovis quickly.

'Thank you, Clovis,' smiled Uncle Rufus. 'Anyway, Anwaar, like me, was keen and excited. As it happens, a little too excited. One night we thought we had Jack cornered. We were trying to trap him with one of the inventions I'd designed for SPI. But it didn't work. Anwaar and I became trapped by Jack. I remember his spirit climbing out of the containment box I had invented, which proved to be useless in Jack's case. We had nothing else. Jack's ghost was crawling closer and closer to us and then Anwaar just ran. He was clearly terrified, as was I, but I couldn't believe he had just run off and left me. Fortunately for me, Jack had other plans and mysteriously dematerialised into thin air.'

'This Anwaar doesn't sound like a good friend to me,' said Tom.

'I agree,' said Eve.

'I'd never leave my friends like that. I would never betray them,' muttered Tom.

'Sounds to me like you're better off without him, Professor,' said Clovis.

'Where is he now?' asked Eve.

'That's a good question. Nobody knows. I haven't seen him for years. The inspector told me she'd heard he had gone back home to Syria. It's a shame, we worked well together and I liked him a lot.'

Tom began to noisily scrape some chocolate spread onto his toast and said, 'Well, Detective Inspector Rutherford seems to think we can help the ghost children. We're not even going to go after Jack.'

'Yeah, she did,' added Clovis, sitting down next to Uncle Rufus.

'I understand that,' said Uncle Rufus. 'But it's the way Mr Wilson described those children to me. They sounded very frightened — the spirits of children who are in that state are not the easiest ghosts to help. It can often become very upsetting for the investigator. As for the ghost of Jack the Ripper, well, I don't know. He's too close by. I'm not happy about it.'

'OK, how about this . . .' Eve slid into a seat at the kitchen table and took a bite out of her toast. 'The first sign of the ghost of Jack the Ripper, we promise we leave.'

Uncle Rufus sighed and looked at the three friends one by one. Each of them returned the look with a wide, persuasive grin.

'It might not be that simple,' he said.

'Look, Uncle, you'll be with us, and you're the one who bound him last time. You're the best teacher in the business. We promise if he shows up, we'll leave him to you. But we really want to help those poor ghost children.'

Uncle Rufus sighed. 'All right, you win.'

Now that the deal was agreed, the friends all felt part of something, something special, something they'd been chosen for. They all knew, including Uncle Rufus, that they were about to embark on an extraordinary adventure. They realised they would be tested, but ultimately it would be worth it if they could help the ghost children.

The only person who was feeling a little lost and vulnerable was Tom. He was excited to be involved, of course. He wanted, *needed* to feel part of something. But he was missing his mum terribly. He'd tried ringing her but her phone had gone to voicemail. Was she missing *him* at all? He didn't want to go home if she wasn't there. He would try to stay here with Eve and the professor for as long as he could. He had to. Just the thought of going back to his dad and that tiny, lonely house, made him feel sick to his stomach. He began to visualise the ghostly children, lost and alone, and in that moment, he knew how they felt. Tom was determined to help them.

'*Mmm* . . . I wonder,' said Uncle Rufus suddenly. 'Let's go and do some digging, kids. Something has just come to me.'

Everyone followed him into the front room, keen to know what the professor had on his mind. He went straight to one of the many bookshelves that covered the ancient uneven walls, jumping up two rungs of a ladder that rolled across the floor on little castors; he propelled himself along, walking his hands across the hundreds of novels, manuscripts, encyclopaedias and maps he had collected over the years. Uncle Rufus was now deep in concentration. With his head bent to one side, he began to shout out various titles and authors as he searched across a long line of old, battered books, his finger gliding slowly along the spines. He stopped suddenly and cried out, 'Aha! Here it is!' He pulled out a rather large green hardback book entitled *The Ripper of Whitechapel* by S. Ward and jumped down off the ladder.

Tom, Clovis and Eve huddled around and watched him flick through the old musty pages.

'Look here.' He ran his fingers along a chapter heading: 'Murder in Dutfield's Yard'. 'Clovis, get on the laptop and see if Dutfield's Yard, Whitechapel, is still there and if so, what buildings are on it.'

'What is it, Uncle?' asked Eve.

'It's just a hunch, my dear girl. When I researched Jack last time, I seemed to remember that some of the street names where he committed his murders had been changed. The school that we are going to visit tomorrow is on a Henriques Street, and I remember that name for some reason. I'm sure it's connected with one of the murders.'

Clovis jumped to it, pulled his laptop from his backpack and began a map search.

Uncle Rufus started to read aloud from the book, more to himself than the others. 'On the thirtieth of September eighteen eighty-eight, the body of Elizabeth Stride (more commonly known as 'Long Liz') was discovered by a delivery man guiding his horse and cart into Dutfield's Yard. The yard was situated just off Berner Street. The deceased was murdered by a cut to her throat with a sharp instrument. No other marks or incisions similar to the other victims of the Ripper were apparent.'

'Oh, poor woman,' whispered Eve.

'Many people believe it was the work of Jack, who was disturbed and couldn't finish off his ritual killing, and so he went on to kill another woman that night.'

Uncle Rufus sat down in his comfy armchair, rubbing his chin, deep in concentration.

'Here it is!' cried Clovis. 'You're right, Professor. The name of the street has been changed. It used to be called Berner Street but it's now called Henriques Street . . . and guess which building sits where Dutfield's Yard, the yard where Elizabeth's body was discovered, used to be?' Everyone rushed over to where he was sitting on the sofa and peered at the laptop. It showed an aerial view of Henriques Street and on it, there in plain sight, was a modern-looking building and to one side, what looked to be a children's playground.

Uncle Rufus stared intently at the image and whispered, 'It's Mr Wilson's primary school.'

CHAPTER 9

A Doll and a Burn

After an early night, Clovis arrived at Eve's house the following morning. He was surprised to see his two friends up, dressed and breakfasted all before nine o'clock.

'Aha, Clovis, my dear boy. Good you're here,' shouted Uncle Rufus from the very top of the staircase.

Boris was so excited to see Clovis that he bolted all the way down the old uneven stairs to greet his friend. Unfortunately for the little English bulldog, Mr Pig the parrot squawked and flapped his wings, landed on the dog's back and began to swear loudly. Boris did not appreciate that. He decided to suddenly stop mid-run, dragging his chubby bottom along the floor, his hind legs held up high to his ears. Once he had thrown off his hitchhiker, he rolled over onto his back and let out a stream of deafening farts, his back legs waggling with the sheer force of the explosions.

Mr Pig retorted by squawking, 'Shut your face! Arse!'

Eve and Tom came into the hallway from the kitchen, laughing at the bird, the dog and the shocked look on Clovis's face.

'They really don't like each other, do they?' said Clovis.

'They will, but it's funny watching them trying to out-do each other. Ready to go?' smiled Eve.

'Yeah, can't wait,' said Clovis.

'Right, all ready?' said Uncle Rufus, taking the last few stairs down into the hallway.

Everyone made their way out into the bright, warm day. They decided to walk to the school, as it wasn't that far away from their estate. After a steady stroll, they soon arrived outside the main gates of the primary school.

'It's weird to think that over one hundred years ago, a woman was murdered here,' said Eve, looking about her.

The building was modern, ugly, with sharp angles and lots of steel. The playground was on the right-hand side. Painted markings of circles and hopscotch squares decorated the black tarmac.

To the left of the school, several diggers stood still like sleeping monsters, waiting to scoop up and gobble the mounds of sand and earth that were piled up high.

'Now that's interesting,' murmured Uncle Rufus, pointing at the building site.

'Could the building work have triggered some paranormal activity?' asked Tom, remembering something the professor had told them when they had begun to delve into the world of hauntings.

'Yes, but why would that be?' asked Uncle Rufus, smiling fondly at Tom.

Clovis was about to answer but Eve gave him a look. Clovis had a habit of interrupting and Tom was going through a hard time at the moment. Eve wanted him to feel involved in the case. Clovis understood the look and stopped himself.

'Lots of people who suddenly notice strange things happening in their home, detect the activity during or just after some kind of building work has been done,' said Tom. 'In some cases, hauntings can begin when a person moves into a new home. No one knows the reason behind it but many think it's because the ghosts see the building as it was in their time, when they were alive, and they don't like it being disturbed, so they start scaring the crap out of people.'

'Brilliant answer, Tom, but less of the "crap". You've been spending too much time with Mr Pig, I think,' laughed Uncle Rufus.

'So you think the diggers might have disturbed something, Uncle?' asked Eve.

'They may indeed have. Come on, let's go and meet Mr Wilson.' Uncle Rufus pressed the buzzer on the gates. They waited a few seconds then suddenly the gates opened automatically. A nervous-looking man wearing a crumpled grey suit was waiting for them at the main entrance. His face was pale and his tired eyes flicked about wildly as if expecting to find someone hiding in the bushes. Uncle Rufus followed the nervous man's gaze, only to see the diggers had started up. They lumbered slowly back and forth, eating away at the hard, scorched ground.

'Professor Pepper?' asked the teacher.

'Yes. Mr Wilson?'

'Indeed. Come in . . . please.' Mr Wilson opened the door wide and smiled weakly as he let everyone inside.

Uncle Rufus stuck his hand out to shake, but just as Mr Wilson was about to take it, something caught Uncle Rufus's eye. It was a man dressed in dark clothing, unusual for the hot weather. Whoever it was, was on the other side of the gates. Uncle Rufus craned his neck and peered closer through the glass door, but they had disappeared.

'Everything all right, Professor?' asked Mr Wilson nervously.

'Oh, yes. Sorry. Just thought I'd seen someone I knew. Never mind. Nice to meet you, and please let me introduce my assistants. This is Clovis, Eve and Tom.'

'Nice to meet you all. Gosh, you're young,' he said, looking at the teenagers. 'But Detective Inspector Rutherford tells me you are experienced in this kind of field.' Clovis, Eve and Tom looked at each other and smiled.

'Shall we get straight to it? I can show you where it all happened. The inspector said you would need to walk through the place where I encountered them.' Mr Wilson was gabbling away. It was clear he was very nervous. Little beads of sweat had appeared on his forehead and he continually patted them with a white handkerchief. He showed everyone around the school, leaving out the loft and the cellar as, according to Mr Wilson, they were much too dark and messy to go into. Eventually he led them back to the corridor where he had first heard and seen the children running away, then he took them to the classroom where he'd seen the ghostly children and encountered 'something so vile, so horrible'. At this point of the tour, Mr Wilson went very white and began to shake. Uncle Rufus suggested they go back to his office.

After the teacher had had a drink of water, he took a deep breath and tried to relax.

Uncle Rufus asked him to take them through the events slowly one more time. From behind the safety of his desk, Mr Wilson began to feel a little better and started to recount his ghostly experience.

'It was the noises, first. I thought some children were mucking about, you know, not gone home for the holidays. I followed the sound of their singing and laughter up the corridor. That sound will haunt me till the day I die. When I got to the end of the corridor, I turned into the furthest classroom on the right. I was ready to give the kids a right telling off. I got the shock of my life, I can tell you. The children were in the classroom all right, but not the sort of children I was expecting. Mrs Kirby, that's the other teacher I mentioned, Professor, she told me about the ghosts of children, but I just thought she was making it up. She's a nice lady, but a bit of an attention seeker. I wish I'd listened to her, I can tell you. Anyway —' Mr Wilson took another gulp of water, followed by a deep breath and continued — 'the

girl was standing alone, but the boy, he was . . . he was . . .'
Mr Wilson began to shake.

'It's all right, Mr Wilson,' said Eve. She kneeled down beside him and took his shaking hand in hers. 'We understand. All of us here have seen ghosts. It's a frightening experience. But we believe you. Let us help you.' She nodded gently and squeezed his hand. The kind gesture seemed to reassure him. He blew out a long stream of breath and, squeezing Eve's hand tighter, he carried on.

'The boy was rocking to and fro in the corner, so sad, so alone. He was only a baby really . . .' He broke off again and closed his eyes tight as if trying to push the memory of it out of his mind once and for all.

'What happened next?' whispered Uncle Rufus. After a long pause and a worried look between Clovis, Tom and Eve, Mr Wilson continued.

'The girl . . . it was extraordinary . . . she was soaking wet, and so was the boy.' Mr Wilson's voice began to shake again. 'I wanted to see if they were solid. I put my hand out and then the girl . . . she looked so angry, she looked as if she were trying to protect herself and the boy. She was trying to hit me, but I couldn't feel anything. Then . . . the look of terror on their little faces. I could see they were scared of something and they suddenly ran away, disappeared into thin air. Out of nowhere *he* arrived like a devil, a monster. It was *evil*. I felt like my heart was going to smash out of my chest. His eyes were red, like hot coals, and he had a . . . a . . . bag.'

89

The teacher put his hands over his eyes, and his words became muffled as he stuttered them out. 'The man opened his bag and brought out a metal rod, it reminded me of some strange-looking medical instrument, you know the kind they use in surgeries. He pushed it towards my face. I remember the smell of sulphur and the heat . . . it was so bright, red-hot, pulsating near my skin. He seemed to be enjoying my fear and when he drew closer, his mouth got wider and wider, I swear I thought he was going to devour me. Oh, but when he laughed, I thought my heart would stop. It was a terrible nightmarish sound. I never want to hear it again. And suddenly it was cold, really really cold, like you wouldn't believe. I was sure my bones were turning to ice, then my arm began to get very hot. I looked down and realised he had pressed the silver rod onto my skin and he . . . he had burned me!' Mr Wilson shouted the last words.

Everyone stared in horror as the teacher rolled up his sleeve and showed a mark that was red and deep, burned into his arm.

'Oh my God!' whispered Eve. She stood up quickly, covering her mouth with her hands.

'Bloody hell!' cried Clovis. He moved towards Mr Wilson to get a better look. 'That looks like a pattern. It's as if something has branded you.'

'I know,' whispered Mr Wilson. 'I thought that myself. What do you think, Professor?' Mr Wilson looked to Uncle Rufus, who was staring intently at the burn mark.

'I think you're right. It *is* a brand mark. I've seen it before somewhere.'

The mark was a figure of eight on its side, and from the centre a cross rose upwards but with two cross lines rather than one. It was about ten centimetres long and five centimetres wide. The burn was deep red, almost black. It reminded Clovis of a seared piece of steak.

'Would you mind if I took a picture of it?' Uncle Rufus asked.

'Of course. Anything to help.' Mr Wilson rolled his sleeve further up and held his arm still while Uncle Rufus took pictures on his phone from various angles.

If Eve, Clovis and Tom hadn't had their own paranormal experience last year, there was no way they would have believed Mr Wilson. They would have thought him mad and delusional, but they had seen the truth now. They knew ghosts were real, they had experienced them first-hand. But this was different ... They had never seen burn marks before. Was that possible?

'You do believe me, don't you?' Mr Wilson looked wide-eyed at the group in front of him. 'The inspector said you would. Can you help me? I'm so afraid that beast will follow me home. I haven't slept since it happened.'

'Of course we believe you,' said Eve warmly.

'What happened after the burning?' asked Uncle Rufus gently.

'I don't know, I lost consciousness. I woke up to find a

paramedic and the school caretaker standing over me. Do you think I'm in danger? What does this burn mean? Am I safe at home? Who will he attack next? He needs to be stopped.' Mr Wilson had tears in his eyes.

'Mr Wilson.' Uncle Rufus's voice was a whisper. He was standing close to the teacher and he put his hand gently on his shoulder. 'The burn is a common sign of activity left by negative entities. You are in no danger at home. This creature is connected to the children you saw and, for some reason, this school. I have a feeling the spirits of the children are trapped here. The ghost of the man will not leave here either. It's the children he's after, not you, Mr Wilson. You must go home, do it now and stay there. Don't come back to the school until the inspector tells you it is safe to do so. Leave this to us. Do you understand?'

Mr Wilson nodded slowly and made his way to the office door, defeated and exhausted.

'Mr Wilson, can I ask just before you go, when did the building work start on the school?' asked Uncle Rufus.

'Only a week ago. Is that relevant?'

'Possibly. Also, have the builders unearthed anything unusual, do you know?'

'Yes, as it happens, they have. I've got a few items in my cupboard. I was thinking of making a display of them.' Mr Wilson went over to a large walk-in cupboard and brought out a few old coins, a leather football, an artillery shell casing and a ball of white tissue paper.

Uncle Rufus looked at the items. 'What's in there?' he said, pointing to the tissue paper.

Mr Wilson unwrapped it carefully, revealing a small, old and very dirty-looking doll.

'That's creepy,' whispered Tom, peering closely at its tiny, battered face. The doll's hair, or what was left of it, stood up in matted balls of filth. The remaining faint red material that once would have been its dress was tattered and shredded. The face was glazed and frozen, staring out with its one remaining glass eye.

'Do you think it's connected to the ghost children?' asked Eve.

'Yes, it might be,' said Uncle Rufus, 'but it could also just be a lost doll from any child. There might not be a connection. It's worth getting it checked out and trying to date it when we get home. May we take the doll, Mr Wilson?' asked Uncle Rufus.

'Of course, do what you want with it. I will write down the key code for the school so you can come and go as you wish. The school is all yours, no one else is here.' Mr Wilson wrote down a set of numbers on a small piece of paper and then picked up his bag.

Taking his lead, the others followed him out of the school. They all stood in the sunshine and, after an awkward silence, the teacher shoved out his hand for Uncle Rufus to shake. 'Well, thank you, Professor, and good luck, all of you.'

Giving a final nod, he walked quickly through the gates.

Everyone watched him walk away. As soon as he was far enough in the distance, Uncle Rufus let out a huge sigh.

'What's the matter, Uncle?' asked Eve.

'Listen to me very carefully,' he whispered. 'After hearing and seeing Mr Wilson, I'm more convinced than ever that this investigation is not for you. Detective Inspector Rutherford has made a mistake. I'm ringing her.'

He took his phone out of his pocket and began to call the inspector. Everyone watched in dismay.

'But, Professor, we can't just leave this now.' Clovis was disappointed, to say the least.

'Uncle, you can't drop us. We *need* to help. The inspector believes we can do it. I know we can do it too.' Eve's voice was getting higher in pitch.

'Shush, Eve!' spat Uncle Rufus. 'Please keep your voice down, we don't want half of Whitechapel knowing our business.'

Everyone heard the voice messaging service through the speaker on Uncle Rufus's phone. He decided not to leave a message, switched off his phone and put it back in his trouser pocket.

Speaking in a quieter voice, Uncle Rufus continued: 'I've no doubt you will all be able to help with the case. But it's the violence I don't like. I know this Jack, I know what he's capable of, the terrible things he did when he was alive and the pain he's inflicting even now he's dead. You saw Mr Wilson's arm, I know what that mark is and it's an evil sign. It's the mark of the Beast. That man was a wreck. Tom, Clovis, your parents would *never* forgive me if anything happened to you, and I'd never forgive myself.'

Tom moved towards Uncle Rufus and placed his hand on his arm. 'Please, Professor, I really want to do this. If we can help those children, then surely it would be a good thing. The SPI thought we should try. Those children must be so scared, so alone. Please, we have to do *something*.'

Uncle Rufus looked into Tom's eyes and saw that he was getting a little upset. He sighed, and with a heavy heart began to pace back and forth. The others said nothing, waiting for a decision.

'All right, but I'm not happy, not happy at all. You can investigate this case, but you are only to deal with the children. Understood? One sign of Jack's ghost, and you leave instantly . . . Yes?'

'Yes, we know that, Uncle. If there's a sniff of Jack, we leave it to you,' said Eve. 'We get it.'

'Good, right, let's get out of here. We're coming back tonight. Let's hope we can catch these ghosts.'

They made their way home in the hot afternoon sun. People carried on about their daily business, unaware of the teenagers' big secret. Eve shook her head, realising how lucky she was to be a part of something so special. They were about to embark on a serious and quite possibly frightening journey, but she knew they had to help the poor souls of those children. Help them through the door, as the inspector had described it.

Tonight, they were going back to the school. Would they find the children? And would her uncle come face to face with the ghost of Jack the Ripper once more?

CHAPTER 10

A New Invention Called Endeavour

As soon as everyone arrived back at Eve's house, Uncle Rufus ran up the stairs, closely followed by a very excited Boris and squawking Mr Pig.

'Come along, chaps, don't hang about, we've got some packing to do.' Uncle Rufus's voice shouted over the din of barking, chatter and flapping. Clovis, Tom and Eve all beamed and sped up the stairs after him.

They found the professor putting various pieces of equipment into a bag. Torches, night-vision cameras, temperature guns, and Eve's favourite ghost-hunting gadgets, the electromagnetic field meters, EMFs. She loved those small machines, which clicked with electricity and whose little lights flashed when a ghost was near. Tom's favourite device was the tapping board, and he was excited to see it going into the professor's kit bag too. He wondered if the ghosts of the children would be able to knock, spelling out their names. What if they couldn't spell?

Clovis noticed a large object standing in the corner of the

room, covered in a huge white sheet. What on earth had the professor got under there?

Uncle Rufus stopped packing his equipment and walked over to Clovis, who was fidgeting with his hands, clasping and unclasping them. Eve recognised the signs. Her friend was excited about something.

'May I ask what it is, Professor?' said Clovis, nodding up at the big white shape.

Uncle Rufus laughed. He couldn't hide his excitement either. 'I've been keeping it a secret. It's my latest invention, although I've not quite finished it yet, there's still some work to do. But I told the inspector about it a few weeks ago and I suspect that's why she's put us on the case with the children. I'm hoping this little beauty might be just what we need to help those poor little mites.'

'Go on, show us,' pushed Eve.

Uncle Rufus sighed heavily. 'All right . . . lady and gentlemen, I present to you the marvellous, the fantastical, Endeavour!' He pulled the sheet off with a flourish and stood back, admiring his newest ghost-hunting invention.

Boris was beside himself with excitement and began to bark and fart at the same time. Suddenly he grabbed one end of the white sheet and began to roll around in it. Mr Pig flapped about, swearing wildly.

Normally Boris and Mr Pig would have had everyone laughing by now but this time, no one was watching them or interested in what they were doing. This time everyone was interested in something else.

Tom, Clovis and Eve didn't utter a word. They just stood and stared at the most ordinary-looking object to ever inhabit Uncle Rufus's attic.

'It's a . . . wardrobe!' said Tom, looking very disappointed. He tilted his head to one side and pointed to the top. '. . . With a cuckoo clock on the roof.'

'Oh no. Not at all. This is my newest and, dare I say, best invention. I've named it after *HMS Endeavour* which was a Royal Navy ship back in the seventeen hundreds,' said Uncle Rufus. 'It sailed for three years, discovering new lands.' He looked at the wardrobe proudly. It might have looked ordinary but he knew its capabilities.

Clovis interjected: 'That was in Lieutenant James Cook's command, wasn't it? It was the first European ship to reach the east coast of Australia.'

'Correct as usual, Clovis.' Uncle Rufus smiled, clapping Clovis lightly on the back. 'A ship exploring new lands. Do you remember my balloon bike invention?' he asked.

'How could we forget it? Actually, where *is* it?' asked Clovis, looking about the room and realising for the first time that the balloon bike wasn't there. The incredible machine Uncle Rufus was referring to was an invention that Clovis had taken a turn on when they had first been invited up to the professor's sacred attic room. A bike was the main part of the invention but as Clovis had pedalled, it had lifted into the air with the aid of two massive balloons. The balloons were tethered to either end of the bicycle and eventually, with much pedalling, the atmosphere around it and the rider changed. Eve and Tom had been amazed, watching as Clovis had been lifted higher into the air, screaming with surprise towards the ceiling. Sparks of white electricity had flown around him and the bike. When the atmosphere had changed, everyone had witnessed something miraculous. A pencil that had been placed on a special stand in between the handlebars disappeared and then amazingly reappeared.

'Well, I've dismantled the balloon bike,' said Uncle Rufus, 'as I needed some of the parts for this new machine.'

He stroked and patted the plain-looking wardrobe with affection.

'But it doesn't even look the same,' said Eve, her face crestfallen. 'I loved the balloon bike.'

'Don't worry, this is better,' said Uncle Rufus with delight. 'It works on the same principle as the balloon bike. Here . . . if you feel the wardrobe, you will see it isn't made of wood. It is in fact made out of the lightest of materials. I designed it as a wardrobe so it could be stored in any room and not look out of place.'

'It's really smooth,' said Clovis, running his hand up and down its side.

'It almost feels like silk,' said Eve, puzzled.

'What material is it?' asked Clovis. He'd never felt anything quite like it. It looked like a dark wood, maybe walnut, but to touch it — well, he just didn't know what to make of it.

'That, my dear boy, is a material that I have invented. It's the first of its kind. I call it polythrixium. If you like, when our case is finished, Clovis, I will take you through the finer components and how I came to the final material.'

Clovis was beside himself with joy, and his friends nudged each other and giggled, watching him as he tried to contain his excitement.

'That would be wonderful,' squeaked Clovis, grinning from ear to ear.

'I'd rather watch paint dry,' laughed Eve.

'Now, wait till you see this, chaps.' Uncle Rufus manoeuvred everyone to stand to one side of the wardrobe. 'Right, Eve, try to lift it.' Uncle Rufus stood back and smiled at his niece in a mischievous way.

'I can't lift *that*,' said Eve.

'Go on, give it a go,' encouraged Uncle Rufus.

Eve stretched both arms around the side of the big rectangular box, bent her knees and scrunched her face up, in readiness to take the wardrobe's weight. But unbelievably she lifted it up as easily as lifting her bike up over her head.

'Wow! Either you're a lot stronger than I thought or that thing's made out of some seriously strange material,' said Tom, as she placed it back down.

'Now, Clovis, open it up,' invited Uncle Rufus, excited to show off his new toy.

Clovis stepped forward and pulled open both doors. Inside was what appeared to be a unicycle; it sat side-on, on top of what looked like two narrow rail tracks which ran in a circle all around the inside walls. On the outside of the tracks, facing the doors, were tiny triangular copper kites. In front of the unicycle seat was one long handlebar, above which sat a small computer screen and keyboard. At the back of the wardrobe was another wall, this one made of what seemed like glass. Behind it was a small space, wide enough to fit a person, and beyond that was a back door, also made of the glass-like material. A chain hung from the ceiling and stopped just above the computer screen. At the bottom of the chain, a porcelain handle swung gently from side to side, with the word *PULL* in bold black letters.

'Oh wow!' exclaimed Eve.

'This looks interesting, Professor,' whispered Tom. 'What does it do?'

'It is only a prototype. Excuse the toilet flush and the cuckoo clock, they will be changed in time for something far superior. I was going to show it to you when I'd finished it, but now that you're all here . . .'

'Does it work? Is it the same principle as the balloon bike? Does it make things disappear and come back again? You know . . . like the pencil?' asked Clovis.

'It certainly does. During the Victorian era, the Davenport

brothers invented something called a spirit cabinet. Both of them would sit inside with their arms tied and they would call out for the spirits to come and interact with them. Sure enough, all manner of paranormal happenings would occur inside and outside of the cabinet, from spirit voices, sounds, objects moving unaided, to the ultimate goal: the full manifestation of a ghost. Of course, many people believed there to be trickery involved but after trying one out for myself I couldn't believe the results. I actually saw a disembodied head float in front of me! It was extraordinary. So, I took the basic Victorian model and just improved it. My belief is that Endeavour can transport souls, spirits . . . ghosts.' Uncle Rufus looked a little nervous and cleared his throat. 'I've wanted for so long to make a machine that can ultimately help trapped spirits. This machine can, I'm sure, move them from one plane to the other.'

'No!' said Eve. 'Really? So, how does it work?'

Uncle Rufus patted the unicycle seat and said, 'Well, just as with the balloon bike, the atmosphere changes in here when you pedal, and the spirit is attracted to the extremely powerful light that is created by the energy of the rider, the copper and the kites. They emulate the light that ghosts usually pass through to get to the Otherside. The cuckoo clock sounds once, letting me know that a spirit is about to enter. Then the clear door at the back opens, shutting the spirit inside the see-through compartment. I've used a type of material that is super-light and so far, unbreakable. Special

coordinates for the Veil are typed into the computer here —'
he tapped on the small screen, which showed a succession of
numbers and letters — 'which then transport Endeavour to
that designated place. Once the atmosphere is correct, the
cuckoo clock strikes three times, the rider pulls the chain,
and the door at the back opens, releasing the spirit. Then,
using more energy from pedal-power, the machine brings the
rider straight back home. There's still more work to do yet
to iron out a few creases, but on the whole, I'm rather pleased
with it. Would you like me to show you?' Uncle Rufus took
a pair of goggles that were hanging off the end of the
handlebar.

'Yes, please,' said Eve excitedly. 'You're going to the Veil?'

'No, not quite. Somewhere much closer today — but I
want you to see it in action.'

Uncle Rufus positioned the goggles over his eyes.

'It gets very bright inside and a little hot,' he went on.
'Now . . .' he twiddled his fingers in the air as if about to
play a piano. 'Tom, pass me that glass of water.'

Tom went to Uncle Rufus's desk and brought over a half-
filled glass.

'Now, let's say this glass of water is a ghost. It's already
been attracted by the light inside Endeavour. In theory the
ghost will come to the door at the back when the right
atmosphere for the spirit has been created inside the
transparent compartment. Think of it as a pressure chamber.
The back compartment will match the atmosphere outside

of Endeavour. When the right atmosphere, pressure and temperature is reached, the cuckoo clock will then sound once, and only then should you open the door using the chain pull.' Uncle Rufus pulled on the chain and everyone watched as the door opened up silently at the back of the wardrobe. He went round the back, and put the glass of water down on the floor inside the glass compartment. 'Clovis, pull the chain for me.'

Clovis did as the professor instructed and everyone watched again as the door closed. 'Now, I will get onto the bike, put in the correct coordinates and begin to pedal.' Uncle Rufus tapped in a sequence of numbers and letters, and then closed both the front doors.

They heard him shout from inside the wardrobe: 'Stand back!'

A low humming noise began to resonate from within Endeavour; the sounds of hissing and sparking could be heard coming from inside.

'Oh my God! Look!' said Eve, pointing.

'I don't believe it,' said Clovis. The ordinary-looking wardrobe had begun to fade slowly away. Within seconds it had completely disappeared, leaving only some sooty black marks on the floor.

'That's unreal,' whispered Tom.

'Where the hell's he gone?' said Eve, beginning to panic.

The strange calling of a cuckoo echoed up from beneath them.

'I'm down here,' shouted Uncle Rufus.

Immediately everyone rushed out of the door and bolted down the stairs where they eventually discovered Uncle Rufus leaning against the wardrobe in the kitchen, arms and legs crossed in a very relaxed stance but breathing heavily.

'That's insane!' cried Tom.

'No way!' said Eve.

'And the water? asked Clovis, walking round the back of the wardrobe. The glass was still there, the water too.

'Are you all right, Uncle?' asked Eve.

'Yes, I'm fine. Never better. Though I have to say the pedalling does take it out of one. I'm not as fit as I used to be.'

He smiled and leaned forward, placing his hands on his knees.

'Right,' he said, once his breath returned to normal. 'So, let's pretend I've arrived at the Veil and the entrance to the Otherside; the clock calls to tell me the right atmosphere has been reached. I would pull the chain and release the ghost. One thing you must never do is get out yourself.'

'Why, what would happen?' asked Clovis.

'Well, that's just it. I'm not sure. I've never left the inside while it's activated, you see. There are more tests that I need to do yet. I don't know how our human bodies would react under the rigours and strains of a completely different dimension, atmosphere, pressure and possibly time,' he said, listing everything off with his fingers. 'There's still so much to learn. We don't know or understand about all the different dimensions, but I'm working on it. As long as you stay on the cycle, you will be fine. It's the compartment where the water is, that's the space that changes. The main doors must always remain closed. Right, meet you back upstairs.'

Uncle Rufus climbed back onto the cycle, leaned across and pulled the doors closed. The sound of the wheel spinning and speeding up could be heard and soon the wardrobe began to pulsate and fizz, and the rhythmic sound of humming that was presumably made by the kites on the tracks emanated throughout the old house.

Everyone stood back and witnessed once more a simple wardrobe rumbling and sparking in front of them, before disappearing.

'Quick, upstairs!' shouted Eve, leading the way up to the top of the building.

The friends waited in the attic and as expected, they heard the now-familiar humming and spitting noise, followed by the appearance of the faint outline of the wardrobe. Within a second or two it was fully back in the room. Comically the cuckoo sprang out of its little door and chirped three times, which made everyone laugh. Then the doors opened to reveal a mist of fog and steam, and a rather dishevelled-looking professor. His hair was sticking up and his face was blackened with some sort of residue. He pulled the goggles off, reminding everyone of a bewildered-looking panda.

'I've discovered it's always a bit bumpy on the way back,'

said Uncle Rufus. Tom, Eve and Clovis couldn't help it, they burst into fits of laughter. 'Do I look ridiculous?' he asked, wiping his face with his hand.

'That was the most amazing thing ever!' said Eve. 'I can't believe you've created such an incredible machine.'

'Yes, incredible, Professor!' cried Clovis, scribbling away in his trusty notebook.

'It's awesome, is what it is,' whispered Tom.

Uncle Rufus patted the side of the wardrobe and closed both the doors. 'It makes me happy to know that this machine, Endeavour, will be able to help spirits get home. Many of them don't know how to get to the Otherside. As we know only too well, they can wander the mortal plane for centuries, always in search of the brilliant white light. It can be very difficult to get them to cross over.'

'You do realise what you have created, Professor, don't you?' said Clovis, looking concerned.

'Well, yes, I do. Some people would see it as a portal for the living to visit the dead. It could cause chaos. Human beings have always wanted to understand the meaning of life, where we come from and where we go when we die. Hundreds of religions and scientific theories would be blown out of the water, if people were to discover that there are indeed different dimensions to our universe and that they could actually travel there! If mankind could use this machine, it wouldn't be used for good, but for power, wealth and greed. We must never let the outside world know about this invention, others like it, the SPI or all of its work. I've shown it to you because I trust you implicitly, and I hope in time you will learn to use it to transport spirits yourselves.' Uncle Rufus looked serious all of a sudden, almost afraid. He took his old-fashioned glasses off and cleaned them using the corner of his beloved old cardigan, his brow furrowed deep in concentration. The enormity of his creation weighed on him suddenly. 'This must never get into the wrong hands,' he said, almost to himself.

'Well, it won't,' said Eve, putting her hand on his shoulder. She had a sudden thought. 'Uncle, shouldn't it be at SPI? Endeavour would be much safer there. Don't you think?'

'Yes, you're right. Now that Detective Inspector Rutherford knows about it, she wants me to test it with a ghost, a willing one. We're thinking of asking Percival, remember him, the guardian? Once the initial experiment has been completed and deemed successful then Endeavour can go off to SPI's headquarters. I will then work on it some more in their laboratory, go through some final tests. When it's complete I will bring you to see the finished machine.'

'That would be fantastic, Professor,' said Tom.

'But hang on,' interrupted Clovis. 'If you can send spirits to the good place, can you take them to the bad too?' He had stopped scribbling in his notebook and was clicking the top of his pen in and out.

'Yes. It can do exactly that. But I certainly will not be journeying to the Abyss. I think the inspector has someone else in mind to do that job. She has a new demon hunter arriving soon apparently. She intends to get their help with Jack, I think. No, I have only put the coordinates into the machine for the Veil.'

'Oh, thank God for that!' Eve sighed, relieved that her uncle wouldn't be making any journeys to the mouth of hell.

'Who else knows of Endeavour's existence?' asked Tom.

'Only the inspector, although you are the first to see it in action. Plus,' he said, leaping into action once more, 'I've constructed Endeavour so the whole thing can be packed down into a suitcase. Watch this.' He pulled on one of the wardrobe's doorknobs and everyone watched in amazement as the machine began to fold in on itself.

As the final door folded and slid into place, the whole thing became the size of a large suitcase.

'It's basically the weight of a unicycle. I've even built a handle, so it's easy to carry.' As if the machine were listening, out popped a large leather handle. 'And wheels on the bottom, so you can pull it along.' Again, two sets of wheels sprang out on either side of the bottom of the case.

'This is all so incredible, Professor. I can't quite believe it.' Clovis's glasses had steamed up with the excitement of it all, his scribbling frenzied as he tried to take down as much information as possible.

Eve, on the other hand, looked worried and scared.

'What's the matter, my dear?' asked Uncle Rufus.

'It's just the thought of you alone inside that thing with

all sorts of spirits. It could be dangerous. What if it breaks down on one of your test runs?'

'It hasn't and it won't. As I said, as long as you never leave the main part of the wardrobe, you are safe. My darling girl, I will be all right.' Uncle Rufus hugged his niece and kissed the top of her head. 'I promise you. I won't put myself in any danger.'

'Promise?' Eve whispered.

'Promise,' answered Uncle Rufus.

'How does Endeavour open up?' asked Clovis, bending over the wooden suitcase. He was just about to touch the handle when Uncle Rufus sucked in his breath.

'Uh-uh!' said Uncle Rufus, shaking his head at Clovis.

'Sorry, Professor. I didn't think.' Clovis snatched his hand away and felt his cheeks burn. He had forgotten the professor's golden rule: never touch any of his inventions without his say-so.

'It's all right, Clovis, it's only because you don't know what you're dealing with yet. In time you will learn how to use all of my inventions, because I won't be with you on all your investigations in the future.'

The three friends looked at each other, a little shocked at the confession.

Uncle Rufus chuckled. 'Don't look so worried, that won't be for a long while yet.'

Clovis and Eve smiled and Tom let out a huge sigh of relief. Boris farted, and Mr Pig, who had been asleep through the whole thing, jumped awake with the fright of Boris's thunderous bottom explosion and screeched a very rude word.

'I think elocution lessons are needed for that bird, and Boris needs the vet,' laughed Uncle Rufus. 'Right, to get Endeavour up, all you do is push down on the suitcase handle. Eve, want to do the honours, my dear?'

Eve leaned over the machine and pushed down on the handle, then quickly jumped back. Three seconds later the wooden suitcase sprang into life before their eyes. It rose up to its full height, unfolding bit by bit. The corners clicked into place with ease. It reminded Tom of a convertible car, all the parts moving robotically into place. Within ten seconds an ordinary-looking wardrobe was back up and ready to be used again.

'And to close it, Tom, do you remember what to do?' Uncle Rufus asked.

Tom nodded. He pulled on the doorknob and stepped back as the wardrobe folded once more into an unassuming brown suitcase.

CHAPTER 11

A Set of Wet Footprints and Some Singing

The school looked different at night. The moon was at its fullest. It peeked in and out between wispy white clouds, throwing milky shadows over the modern building.

Everyone had helped to unload all the ghost-hunting equipment from Uncle Rufus's little Mini.

Boris sat on the pavement, his ears pricked. Something had caught his attention.

'What are you looking at, boy?' asked Eve, patting her dog's head. She looked across at the school, trying to tell what had caught his eye but she could see nothing.

Once through the automatic gates, Uncle Rufus led the way to the main front door. 'Now remember, no matter how much you may be tempted to turn the lights on, you mustn't. No one must know we are here. That's a direct order from Detective Inspector Rutherford.' Uncle Rufus set his bag of kit down and turned to the three friends. 'And, most importantly, if we make contact with the ghost of Jack, you are to leave immediately.' Everyone nodded in agreement.

'I think I can speak for us all, Professor,' said Tom, 'when I say that we are very happy to leave the ghost of a Victorian serial killer to you.'

Uncle Rufus smiled as he tapped out a series of numbers on the keypad. Instantly the main door clicked open.

'All right? Are we all ready?' Uncle Rufus asked.

'Ready as we'll ever be,' whispered Clovis, pushing his glasses up the bridge of his nose.

'Let's go in then,' grinned the professor.

When they had visited the school that morning, the reception area had seemed friendly, welcoming and bright. Now, as Eve shone her torch around the small room, it felt oppressive and creepy. Children's spattered paintings of faces, wobbly crayon trains and houses bore down on them. A crocodile made out of eggboxes ran eerily down the length of one of the walls, its teeth ready to bite and chew any victim. Something so innocent and pure now suddenly felt so wrong. Eve was very uneasy.

'Now, one thing to consider,' said Uncle Rufus, looking about him, 'it's been a very hot day, the building will make all sorts of strange noises, creaks and groans as it cools down.'

'You mean, don't assume every noise is a ghost,' said Clovis with confidence.

'Precisely,' said Uncle Rufus, grinning at his protégé.

Clovis hoped his confident demeanour would hold up for the rest of the night. Inside he was a little nervous. He couldn't get the image of Mr Wilson's burn mark out of his head. His mum, who was a total believer in all things supernatural, had always told him, 'It's the living that can hurt you, not the dead.' But after seeing Mr Wilson's arm . . . well, that had unnerved him.

Suddenly Boris gave one loud bark, which made everyone jump.

'Argh, Boris!' screeched Eve, clutching her chest, her breath seemingly having left her whole body at once.

'He's sensed something,' whispered Uncle Rufus. 'Quick, set up the equipment along the corridor and then let's head into the classroom where Mr Wilson encountered the ghosts.'

Everyone got to work. Several night-vision cameras were set up, taking in different angles of the corridor. All of them were now switched on and recording. Three electromagnetic field meters were placed on the floor, a good space between each one. Their lights remained red, meaning nothing was interfering with the fields. Two temperature guns on little tripods sat in the reception area, pointing down the corridor; they both showed normal readings for the building. Everyone had a tiny night-vision camera clipped to their utility vests so that every move they made could be recorded. All the footage and data would be analysed after the investigation, first by Uncle Rufus, and then the inspector. She would take all the recorded findings and store it safely at the SPI headquarters.

'EVP watches are synced and switched on?' asked Uncle Rufus. 'Hopefully they will be just as successful at capturing any ghosts' voices as when we used them the last time,' he said, tapping his watch's face.

Everyone checked the watches that Uncle Rufus had given to them on the night of their first investigation with him. They were treasured possessions. They recorded the voices of the dead. Only when the watches were connected to Messenger One, one of the machines in the professor's attic, were the ghost hunters able to hear exactly what had been captured.

'All set,' replied Tom.

'Set,' said Clovis.

'Set,' added Eve.

'Right, let's head towards the classroom. Our aim is for you to connect with those poor children and for me to find out if the ghost of Jack is really here.' Uncle Rufus strode with purpose, his posture straight and proud, as if he were about to go into battle.

Boris led the way down the corridor, sniffing as he went. Suddenly he stopped abruptly, the fur all along his back standing up like porcupine quills. His growls rumbled and grumbled deep within his throat. The bulldog's eyes were glued to a spot at the end of the corridor.

'Here we go,' whispered Eve. A shot of adrenalin rushed through her. Yes, she was nervous, scared, even . . . but wow! She loved this, loved being with her best friends and her uncle, investigating ghosts.

A troubling noise resounded from above them. Footsteps,

little footsteps, running and bouncing along. Everyone slowly looked up.

'That definitely came from upstairs,' said Clovis worriedly.

'There's an upstairs?' gulped Tom.

'Well, there's this floor, a cellar and a loft space apparently,' said Uncle Rufus, shining his torch onto the ceiling. 'Mr Wilson mentioned them, remember?'

'Well, we know no one else is in the building, don't we?' whispered Eve.

'Unless of course there's some children hiding up there,' replied Clovis sarcastically.

'Well, I for one won't volunteer to go up and have a loo—'

Tom's sentence was interrupted by the ominous sound of a child singing.

> *Ring-a-ring o' roses,*
> *A pocket full of posies . . .*

The strange, creepy noise was accompanied by the odd discordant note of a piano. Ordinarily the singing might have sounded sweet, innocent, even, but right now, in the darkness of the empty school, it sounded haunting and spooky.

Everyone had crouched down for some strange reason, perhaps feeling safer that way. Their backs were against the walls of the corridor.

'*A-tishoo . . . a-tishoo . . . We all fall . . . down . . .*' The last words faded into the distance.

'Where's that singing coming from?' whispered Clovis, glancing about.

'The running above us has stopped and Boris hasn't moved from his spot. Look at him,' said Eve, stroking his back. The little bulldog was still staring at something at the end of the corridor, but the growling had ceased and his hackles were down. Suddenly he cocked his head to one side and sat down, as if someone were talking to him, giving him commands.

'Something is definitely at the end of the corridor,' said Uncle Rufus. 'Hello, can you see us?' he asked gently. Standing up, he slowly began to walk forward. Everyone followed as quietly as they could.

A very loud noise rang out all around them: *BANG!*

It sounded like a door being slammed shut. The whole place shuddered with the vibration as if a bomb had exploded. Immediately everyone dropped to their knees. Boris began to bark, his little front paws lifted off the ground: he meant buisness.

The pitter-patter of running feet rushed right down the corridor straight past them all.

Eve clicked her torch on and shone it down the end of the corridor. She could have sworn she caught a glimpse of a white shadow flitting into the classroom on the right-hand side.

'I think the children are in the classroom,' she said. As she switched her torch off, she noticed her hand was shaking. Her uncle must have seen it, as he gently put his own over hers to steady her.

'The cameras have hopefully caught the images. Let's go further towards the classroom.' Uncle Rufus stood up, dusted his trousers down and began to walk forwards. The others followed but weirdly Uncle Rufus stopped suddenly: the sound of something splashing seemed to be coming from the floor.

'Is that water?' asked Tom, clicking on his torch. The bright circular light illuminated a shimmering pool of water. The floor's surface seemed to be moving underneath their feet. Uncle Rufus tapped his foot up and down, sending splashes spraying up into the air.

'What the hell!' exclaimed Tom, shining his own torch about him.

'Where has it come from? This water wasn't here when we set up the equipment,' said Clovis, confused.

'There doesn't seem to be a leak either,' said Uncle Rufus, flashing his torch at the ceiling and the walls.

'Look at this,' said Eve. Everyone followed her beam of light and was shocked to discover two sets of wet footprints. One was smaller than the other. They had seemingly appeared from nowhere.

Uncle Rufus and Clovis instantly began to take lots of photos of the footprints. They were of bare feet, no shoes.

'These definitely belong to children. Here, Clovis, take a picture with my torch lying alongside them for a size reference.' Clovis did as the professor said, and it wasn't long before they had exhausted every possible angle photographing the puddle footprints.

'How is that possible, Professor?' asked Tom. 'How can a ghost leave physical remains of themselves like these footprints?'

'It's something that intrigues me too, Tom, but as we know from our experiments with Endeavour, water does seem to be able to travel and pass through different planes. What I want to know is, how old is this water? Does it come from their time? Here, help me collect some, put it in this bottle.' Uncle Rufus passed a small plastic container to Tom, who carefully scooped up some of the water from the prints.

'Perfect, now take another bottle and put some water from the other footprint in there.'

Tom did as instructed and he passed the little bottles back to Uncle Rufus, who in turn placed each bottle inside a plastic bag and put them into his rucksack.

'We shall analyse these back home. It will be interesting to see if there's anything unusual about this water.' Uncle Rufus was pleased. Already they were getting somewhere. He couldn't wait to get back to his attic and begin the various tests.

'I hope we can help, Professor?' said Clovis.

'Of course, my dear boy. I want you all to learn as much as you can.'

They followed the watery footprints down the rest of the corridor and arrived inside the classroom. Everything looked as it should. There were little chairs set on top of the tables, a whiteboard in the corner, books, plastic boxes filled with wooden bricks and coloured pencils, and all the other items one would expect to find in the classroom of a primary school. But one thing that wasn't present was the ghosts of two children.

Eve stepped into the centre of the room and nervously began to call out to the children: 'Hello? Don't be frightened, my name's Eve and we've come to help you.' She turned slowly, her head tilted upwards, her eyes closed. No one said a word.

They watched Eve call out again and again, her voice getting louder and louder but nothing happened. Boris lay down on the floor and let out an explosive fart.

'That's one way to kill the atmosphere. You've probably scared them off with your rear end, Boris,' said Clovis with disappointment.

'You can say that again,' said Tom, holding his nose.

'Where did they go?' asked Eve. She was frustrated. She checked her own EMF meter and saw nothing was showing up. Boris was very happy and chilled, so much so, he had lain down and actually fallen asleep, little snores rolling around in the back of his throat. It seemed calm and peaceful in the room; there didn't seem to be any evidence of paranormal activity. Eve was convinced the ghosts had come this way though. She'd *seen* one of them, and their footprints led here. Why didn't they want to talk?

'Maybe that's it for tonight,' said Clovis, relaxing a bit. He took one of the little chairs off the table and sat on it.

He looked ridiculous sitting there, like a giant, his enormously long legs folded up beneath him. 'Perhaps we need to chill. They are children, after all. They might be scared of us.' Clovis crossed his arms and smiled.

'Clovis is right,' said Uncle Rufus. 'Let's just sit here and wait for a while.' He took down another small chair and sat down.

They all stared in silence, looking and listening for something to happen, anything at all.

'Right,' sighed Uncle Rufus. 'I think we should split up. Clovis, you stay with me. Tom and Eve, you take Boris and see if you can find a way into the loft space. I think given that we heard the children running above us, it makes sense that you head up there.' Eve clicked a lead onto Boris and huddled close to Tom. 'And, Tom, Eve: remember the first sign of anything negative, you get out. Understood?'

'Understood,' they chorused.

'Where are you and Clovis going?' added Eve warily.

'Well, we'll go into the music room, that's where I presume the piano playing and singing came from. We'll meet back here in twenty minutes.'

Clovis, Tom and Eve stood completely still. Nerves had clearly got the better of them.

'Go on, then,' laughed Uncle Rufus. 'You want to be ghost hunters, don't you?'

Eve and Tom nodded.

'Well, go hunting, then,' said Uncle Rufus.

Tom and Eve made their way back down the corridor, heading towards the reception area.

'I'm thinking,' whispered Eve, 'that maybe the stairs to the loft are inside the reception office. What do you think?'

Tom gripped Eve's hand tightly. 'Let's go and see.' He followed her closely, turning around constantly to check no one was behind them.

'Why do *we* get the creepy loft?'

'*You* know why. The professor always says we cover more ground by splitting up. We might get more activity caught on our equipment and we'll finish the investigation quicker. It's one of the first rules of an investigation. You know when we get tired, we can make mistakes. I suppose he's right, maybe the ghosts of the children *are* upstairs. Here, look, the office.' They had come to a door behind the reception desk. Tom turned the handle. They walked inside and at the back of the room their torchlight picked out another door. A glass panel ran along the back wall and through it a blurry set of stairs could be seen leading upwards.

'You were right. Well done. We ready?' asked Tom. He smiled at Eve, determined to show her that he wasn't scared, but secretly hoping his true feelings wouldn't betray him.

Suddenly the *THUMP, THUMP, THUMP* sound of children running came from above. Eve and Tom looked up at the ceiling. Disturbed dust motes twirled and danced down in the torchlight and onto their worried faces.

'Oh my God! I can't believe we're going to go up there.'

Tom's voice was barely audible. Eve hadn't seen her best friend so scared before.

'Come on. Let's do it. We'll be all right. The professor and Clovis aren't far away. C'mon, Tom. I promise we'll be fine.' Eve couldn't believe she was being so brave.

'Sorry, it's just we've seen so much already. When you know that ghosts are real, I think it gets scarier. You, me and Clovis, well, we've seen them up close, haven't we? That whole experience last Halloween was one that I'll never forget. I think the more you see and feel and hear, the more frightened you get. I suppose it's Mr Wilson's story, too, that has bothered me. He looked so frightened.'

'I know what you mean, but we want to do this, don't we? I know I do,' said Eve. She was trying so hard to be brave but little by little her nerve was beginning to waver. The longer they stood at the bottom of the stairs, the more chance she'd bottle it.

'You're right. Let's do this.' Tom pushed past Eve and with a renewed surge of positivity opened the door and began to climb the stairs, closely followed by Eve and a reluctant Boris. Boris wasn't keen on climbing, he preferred flat ground. It meant his sturdy little legs had to work that bit harder. The stairs were steep, dark and eerie, and as they all got closer to the top, they heard what sounded like a child giggling. Tom, Eve and Boris instantly stopped moving and stood completely still.

'Did you hear that?' Eve's voice was more of a squeak,

her mouth had gone completely dry, her hands tingled and turned wet with perspiration. She pushed a breath out and tried to calm herself down. They waited on the stairs for what seemed an age in hope of hearing the creepy child's laughter again. Even Boris kept still and quiet. But the strange, spooky noise didn't happen again. Tom, Eve and Boris began to move upwards once more and after a couple more steps they arrived at the top.

Tom swept his torch around the small space. The room was filled with filing cabinets; boxes of paper, crayons, old Christmas decorations that the pupils had obviously made spewed out everywhere. Shelves were lined with books and old computers. Paints, pots and brushes collected dust in a corner. Large cobwebs hung like giant nets from the ceiling.

Eve took her EMF meter out and swept it from left to right. Immediately the little device began to crackle with electricity, the lights dancing on the top.

'We've definitely got company,' said Eve. She took a deep breath and called out again. 'Hello, are you up here?'

A small giggle tinkled through the air. It seemed to come from the back of the room.

'Why won't they talk to us?' asked Eve, getting frustrated.

'Maybe they're scared,' said Tom, weaving past the boxes and decorations.

'They don't sound scared to me.'

Now off his lead, Boris followed Tom and promptly sat down as if he'd been given a command.

'Did you see that?' asked Tom. 'It's as if someone is talking to him.'

Boris barked loudly once and then lay down.

All of a sudden, the sound of one of the filing cabinets crashing down onto the floor brought Eve to her knees with fright. It made such a din that her ears hummed. Tom and Boris rushed to her side, then they all heard the terrible sound of a child crying and whimpering. Boris barked once more and sat down obediently, his gaze fixed on someone that neither Eve nor Tom could see.

CHAPTER 12

Annie and Joe Come Out to Play

Uncle Rufus and Clovis were having an interesting time in the music room. It was a small space where a piano took centre stage. On the walls, pictures of famous musicians through the ages stared on, supposedly intended to influence any aspiring young marvel to do their best.

Uncle Rufus was pointing a camera at the piano and Clovis was looking at it intently.

'Please, if you can play the note again.' Clovis was sitting on the floor, never taking his eyes off the piano keys. Already they had witnessed something remarkable. Clovis hadn't thought such things possible but now that he had seen and heard it with his own eyes and ears, he knew a ghost had been playing the piano right in front of him.

A white key in the centre of the piano moved on its own, striking a C note.

'Wow!' cried Clovis. 'It played it, Professor.'

'Ask again, Clovis.' Uncle Rufus was panning the little night-vision camera along the keyboard.

'Thank you, can you play another note?' Nothing

happened at first, all was quiet but then a succession of keys were struck, causing several notes to spill out of the piano. Then suddenly and most alarmingly, the piano hood came slamming down, nearly catching Uncle Rufus's camera and hands inside.

'Are you all right, Professor?' asked Clovis.

'Yes, dear boy. I'm quite all right. A close shave. Wasn't that simply marvellous though?' said Uncle Rufus, grinning from ear to ear. 'We've got it all on camera too. Simply wonderful.'

'I wonder who was playing it?' asked Clovis.

'I think it was one of the children.'

A thunderous crash banged above their heads.

'Quick, Clovis, the loft.'

Uncle Rufus and Clovis ran out of the music room, calling as they went. They ran along the corridor and back into the reception area. Standing still, they waited for the sound of either Tom or Eve to lead them to their whereabouts.

Boris's bark alerted them from a door at the back of the reception office.

'This way!' shouted Uncle Rufus. They both leaped up the steps and arrived in the loft to find Eve and Tom huddled on the floor. A filing cabinet was on its side and Eve was crying.

'Oh, my dear girl, what's happened? Are you hurt?' asked Uncle Rufus.

'It's all right,' said Eve, standing up and wiping her eyes.

'The filing cabinet fell over and then we heard what sounded like a child crying. It was the sound of the crying that upset me. It sounded so awful, so, so sad. We must help them, Uncle, these children, whoever they are. We need to find out why they're here.' Eve sniffed back more tears and her chin jutted out with determination.

'I've got a feeling these children are playing with us,' said Tom.

'I agree,' said Uncle Rufus, 'and one of them has just been playing the piano. We've filmed the keys being pressed down.'

'No way!' exclaimed Tom.

Boris began to bark again but this time he was excited, as if he wanted to play.

'What is it, boy?' asked Eve.

'Listen,' whispered Tom, clicking his torch on.

All around them they could hear the sounds of knocking and tapping.

'I hear it,' said Uncle Rufus. He panned his EMF meter around in an arc and instantly the light display on the top began to flicker brightly.

'Someone is here with us,' said Clovis.

'I don't think they ever left,' said Eve confidently. 'They don't seem to be negative spirits, as our little doggie ghost detector here —' she patted Boris — 'seems to be very happy. I think he can see the children and I think it's their spirits making the knocking noises.'

'I agree,' whispered Tom. 'They're the ones who have

been active so far. It's like they've been sussing us out, to see what kind of people we are.'

Tom suddenly surprised everyone by standing in the middle of the room and talking out loud to the ghosts of the children. He told them more about himself, how he liked to play football, how he loved to spend time with his friends. He asked them if they liked Boris and would they like to play with him.

Everyone stood completely still, listening to Tom and his carefully whispered monologue.

Uncle Rufus had taken his rucksack off and was rummaging inside it. The noise was a distraction and Boris came wiggling over to sniff out what his master was doing. Perhaps there would be a treat?

Uncle Rufus pulled out a ball of tissue and unwrapped the little doll that Mr Wilson had given to them earlier in the day.

'Now let's see if this gets a reaction,' he whispered as he put it carefully on the floor. Next to it, he placed the tapping board, an invention he had perfected and had wonderful results with before. It looked like an electronic board game. It was a small wooden panel, and the letters of the alphabet lined the top of the board and numbers from zero to nine lined the bottom. In the middle, random words sat next to each other, such as *sad*, *excited*, *happy*, *lonely* and *naughty*. Behind each character was a small light, so when the ghost wanted to communicate, they tapped, causing a vibration.

This lit up a letter which triggered a computerised voice to announce the corresponding information. At the end, when the spirit had answered a question or finished a statement, the board would assemble all the letters into words and speak the information out. It was an amazing piece of kit and had helped greatly on their last case. Would the tapping board do the same this time? By the sounds that the spirits were making in the loft, it seemed that the board might just work its magic again.

The knocking and tapping had become more fevered and rapid, so much so that Eve began to feel the vibrations underneath her feet.

'Will you talk to us?' asked Tom. 'Please.'

'Ask two taps for yes, one for no,' reminded Uncle Rufus. Without asking, two loud knocks thumped under Tom's feet.

'Can you see us?' asked Tom, looking about the dark room. He imagined the children, shy and frightened, watching from a dark corner. 'It's all right, we don't mean you any harm. These are my friends. Clovis, Eve and the professor, and of course Boris.' Tom pointed to everyone in turn. I think you like Boris best, don't you?'

Two loud bangs erupted under Tom's feet, causing him to jump back in alarm.

'Bloody hell! That was loud,' Tom said in shock.

Suddenly a little voice whispered in Tom's ear: '*Hello.*'

'Oh, wow! Did you all hear that?' His voice was high-pitched with excitement and nerves.

'Hear what?' asked Uncle Rufus.

'The voice, it was a girl's voice. She just said "Hello" to me.' Tom rubbed his ear as if something had just tickled it.

'I didn't hear anything,' said Eve. 'Did you?' She looked to Clovis, who shook his head.

'Can you come and talk to us all?' asked Tom, turning around, panning his torch about the loft space.

Again, two loud knocks reverberated through the floor.

'I can't believe it, that was so hard it actually tickled my feet,' laughed Tom.

'Well done, Tom, you've certainly made contact,' said Uncle Rufus. 'The fact that one of them whispered in your ear is amazing. She must trust you. Now then, let's see what they have to say. Sit down, everyone. If we can gain their confidence, we may be able to help them.'

They formed a circle around the tapping board and Uncle Rufus placed the little doll next to it. He then turned the device on and it made a tone to let everyone know it was powered up and ready.

'Right, Tom, you're the one the children seem to like. They are responding to you. You ask the important questions.' Uncle Rufus patted Tom's back.

'OK. What shall I ask first?' Suddenly, Tom began to doubt himself.

Clovis nudged his friend in the ribs. 'Go on, mate. You're good at this,' he said, looking above him. 'They seem to like you.'

Tom cleared his throat, took a big breath and began.

'Can you use the board and spell out your names for me?'

Instantly tapping and knocking noises came from under the board and different letters lit up in quick succession. The male automated voice that came out of the board's speaker sounded so creepy. Eve shuddered with the weirdness of it. Then there was a pause, which was a sign that the computer programme had understood a word had been made, and then it proceeded to speak out the message in full.

'Annie . . . Joe.'

Everyone shuffled forward. They had two names now. This was progress. Uncle Rufus's face was beaming in the soft light.

'And how old are you?' asked Tom gently.

The tapping lit up a number eight; a pause, then a number four.

'So, one is eight and one is four?' said Eve.

'I think so,' replied Clovis.

'Is this Annie we're talking to?' whispered Eve.

Two loud knocks could be felt from underneath the floor.

'That's a yes! Hello, Annie, are you eight?' asked Tom.

Again, two loud knocks.

Uncle Rufus leaned forward, picked up the dishevelled little doll and handed it to Tom.

'Annie, is this your doll?' asked Tom gently.

An explosion of knocks thundered all around them. Then silence. Everyone looked to each other, uncertain as to what would happen next. Two clear knocks thudded, signalling that the doll definitely did belong to Annie.

'And is Joe your brother?' whispered Tom.

Two more knocks.

Uncle Rufus sat back and wrapped the doll back up in the tissue paper, placing it carefully into his rucksack. Then he took a deep breath and held his body taut, as if expecting to be hit. 'I'm sorry to ask you this, Annie, but were you murdered?'

There was a long pause. The silence was almost deafening. Tom could hear his heart pounding in his head. The sound of a ghostly child's whimper crept around them.

'Oh my God! Did you all hear that?' asked Clovis, looking around the group.

Everyone nodded that they had.

'Is it me, or is it getting colder?' asked Eve, hugging herself.

She was right. The temperature was dropping rapidly, the bitter air spreading icy fingers throughout the small room, causing everyone's breath to turn into white swirls that slowly twisted in the darkness. Clovis looked at the reading on the temperature gun. 'I can't quite believe how cold it's got and how quickly. It's a warm night, it doesn't make sense. Professor?' Clovis leaned over to where Uncle Rufus was sitting and showed him the digital numbers that illuminated on the gun's screen.

'Minus twelve degrees!' whispered Uncle Rufus. 'I knew it was getting cold but I didn't realise just how much. That's the biggest drop I've ever encountered in a haunting.' Uncle Rufus was in his element. 'Just think of all the phenomena we've hopefully caught so far on the cameras and the EVP watches. This is spectacular! Is everyone all right to carry on?'

Clovis, Tom and Eve nodded. Eve shivered, so Tom kindly took a jumper from his rucksack and passed it to her.

Suddenly the tapping board jumped back into life. The letters flashed, illuminating everyone's transfixed faces. Each letter was spoken out by the eerie computerised voice in quick succession.

'It was going too fast. What did they tap out?' asked Eve.

'Wait for it,' said Uncle Rufus. He leaned further over the board, as if willing it to speak.

The ghost hunters watched, wide-eyed, as they all waited for the computerised voice to talk again, this time putting the letters together to form a sentence.

It suddenly blurted out three words: 'He ... killed ... Mother.'

Eve gasped out loud.

'Did the man who killed your mother kill you?' Uncle Rufus whispered the question. The awful question.

Everyone waited with bated breath for an answer but curiously nothing happened.

'Have they gone?' asked Clovis, looking to Uncle Rufus.

'I don't think so. Tom, try again, they respond better to you,' said Uncle Rufus with urgency.

Tom leaned forward and asked the question again. 'Hello,

Annie, I'm so sorry to ask this question, as I know it must be upsetting, but did the man who killed your mummy kill you?'

Two loud, explosive knocks erupted from the floor once more.

'Who was it?' asked Eve, suddenly angry.

The board flew into a frenzy, tapping and knocking so quickly it was hard to hear what was being communicated.

'I can't make sense of it; it's going so quickly again,' shouted Eve, trying to follow the lights and listen to the machine.

'Shush, everyone,' said Uncle Rufus.

The computerised voice began to talk. 'He . . . was . . . a . . . bad . . . man . . . We . . . saw . . . him . . . kill . . . Mother . . . He . . . took . . . us.'

Eve gasped; Clovis and Tom sat dumbstruck. Uncle Rufus was practically sitting on top of the tapping board.

Then he asked the question they had all been dying to ask. 'Did he tell you his name, Annie?'

Again, the board began to speak out, letter after letter and then the computerised voice spoke.

'. . . Jack . . .'

It was getting colder by the second and the sound of the ghostly children crying began to get louder and louder. Eve pressed her hands to her ears.

'That sound, it's so awful. We need to help them, Professor,' said Tom.

'We will, my dear boy,' said Uncle Rufus. 'All in good time.'

The ghosts of Annie and Joe were obviously distressed and agitated. Tom whispered gently into the dark room, feeling the emotion that these two lost children were experiencing. 'Annie, we can help you, that's why we've come.'

Uncle Rufus urged him on. 'Tell them we can reunite them with their mother. But you must ask Annie *where* they were killed.'

Tom looked at Uncle Rufus for encouragement. He wasn't sure why the professor thought he was the one who could best communicate with them.

Uncle Rufus smiled. 'You *can* help them, Tom. For some reason they feel a connection to you. You can do it.'

Tom furrowed his brow in deep concentration. Taking a breath, he pressed on. 'Let us help you. Can you tell us why you're here?' Tom thought that was a better question. He felt the gentler approach was more appropriate.

His thinking was right, as the tapping board illuminated more letters, which spelled out the words: 'Killed . . . here.'

Then the knocking went crazy again. The singular letters that were vocalised by the computerised voice read out the words: 'Help . . . us!'

'We *will* help you!' shouted Eve desperately. Then more knocks and taps began to spell out another three words that no one in the group would ever forget.

'Jack . . . here . . . *RUN!*'

CHAPTER 13

Uncle Rufus and a Ghost Called Jack

'Quick, everyone. Out now!' shouted Uncle Rufus.

Boris had begun a tirade of loud aggressive barks, his hackles rising like spikes, making him look so much bigger. He snarled and snapped at something at the back of the room. Then suddenly he whimpered and fled as if he'd been struck. He ran as he'd never run before. Everyone watched the rotund dog bolt down the stairs.

'Go, everyone, stay in the reception area. Make sure Boris is all right,' instructed Uncle Rufus.

Tom, Clovis and Eve didn't need telling twice. They ran towards the stairs. Eve, at the back, turned to see her uncle positioning his rucksack in the centre of the room.

'Uncle, please be careful,' she pleaded.

'Don't worry, Eve, I'll be fine. Just wait downstairs for me.' Eve nodded and ran down the stairs, shutting the door firmly behind her.

Uncle Rufus unzipped his rucksack and brought out a wooden chest. He undid two catches on the top and the side of the chest dropped down to reveal an array of glass vials hanging in rows from little silver circular slots, each one filled with special, coloured liquids. Underneath the vials was a small hexagonal box which he took out and placed on the floor directly in front of him. Uncle Rufus drew his finger along the lines of vials and chose one filled with a deep purple liquid. He had been working on a new molecular formula that could break down the essence of a spirit. If this purple liquid worked, it would be a major leap forward for his research on negative entities, a field of work he had been interested in for a long time. He sucked in his breath, unclipped the chosen vial, uncorked it, and waited. Any second now.

As he heard his EMF meter buzzing wildly, he looked up quickly. The room began to get colder still and Uncle Rufus shivered. He knew he had to be quick. Once the ghost of Jack saw the bright light, he wouldn't be able to resist it. No spirit could. Quickly he jabbed his foot down onto the little hexagonal device and immediately a triangle of brilliant white light shot up to the ceiling in a wide V shape. Uncle Rufus shielded his eyes, held his breath and readied himself. Any second now. All he had to do was get Jack into the light and douse him with the new formula. If his calculations were correct, the spirit would hopefully decompose and disappear to the plane he deserved to be in. In Jack's case, it would surely be the Abyss.

Suddenly, Uncle Rufus felt a violent blow to his stomach. All his breath was sucked out of him and somehow, he was flying through the air. He fell backwards and landed heavily on the floor. Taken off-guard, the professor was annoyed with himself for not anticipating such an arrival of the spirit. He knew after all his years of experience that negative spirits could be very violent, and if this one was who he thought it to be, then he should have been far more prepared. He'd met Jack before. He knew what he was capable of.

He shook his head and stood up quickly. He needed to *see* the spirit that was with him, only then could he get him into the light. A deep pain in his neck crippled him. He cried out in agony, the shock nearly buckling his knees, but he held on. Something had taken hold of his neck, something with large, icy-cold hands. He yelled out once more as an invisible force grabbed at his shoulders and dragged him backwards. Was this the ghost of Jack? Uncle Rufus knew it had to be.

He turned around quickly, brought his arm back and fired the purple liquid into the air. All around him the space twisted and rolled into a thick purple misty fog. There, at the back of the room, growing, morphing into a shape that Uncle Rufus recognised instantly, was the ghost of Jack the Ripper.

Down below in the reception area, Clovis checked that Boris was fine and hadn't been harmed. He seemed OK but was now hellbent on trying to get back to his master upstairs.

Clovis tried to calm him down.

Eve and Tom both looked to the ceiling and watched as

flakes of old paint floated down and around them. The bangs and thuds coming from upstairs were terrifying.

'I'm going back up,' shouted Eve.

'No! The professor told us not to,' said Tom, catching her hand.

'But what if he gets hurt badly?'

'He'll be all right. He's the professor,' replied Clovis calmly, who had by chance found an old biscuit in his rucksack. Boris had relented and calmed down long enough to eat the tasty treat. He now sat, leaning against Clovis's leg, licking his lips.

Another huge bang thundered from above their heads. Boris let out a long whimper and everyone looked up.

'I think,' whispered Clovis, as another fleck of paint glided down and rested on top of his head, 'we should stay here, like the professor told us. We go up if we hear that he's in trouble. Agreed?'

Tom and Eve were not happy but nodded.

Professor Rufus Pepper stood face to face with a true creature born out of Hell. The ghostly monster of a man was hideous, his face deformed by evil and wickedness. His clothes were black and Victorian in style: a top hat and dark cloak, and he loomed large over the professor.

All at once, Uncle Rufus felt himself being lifted off the floor before once more being thrown across the foggy room. He landed with a crash into a pile of boxes and lay still, not daring to move a muscle. This formula wasn't working. The ghost of Jack didn't seem interested in the white light, either. For the first time in a long while, Uncle Rufus knew he was in trouble. Once more he was facing the most malevolent force he'd ever encountered and he seemed more powerful than the last time they'd met.

Opening his eyes slightly, he could just make out the ghost walking in an unnatural jerky motion towards him. His body was translucent. He stomped slowly, awkwardly coming closer and closer to him, and in his gloved hand he carried a doctor's bag. Uncle Rufus recoiled in horror as Jack pushed his face towards his: the pain he felt on his skin was horrendous. It was so cold, it hurt. The ghost's eyes burned like red-hot coals and his thin lips twisted into a vile sneer.

Uncle Rufus couldn't move, it was as if a heavy weight were on top of him. He couldn't fight, couldn't get away. He was trapped and didn't want to look any more. He resigned himself to his fate: this time, he knew the monster was going to kill him. He squeezed his eyes tight shut and waited for the final blow. But what came was much worse: a scorching fiery sensation and the smell of burning flesh.

Downstairs, one of the EMF meters in Tom's pocket had screeched into life. Everyone jumped. Tom took it out and scanned the area around them. Suddenly the sound of crying and whimpering came from the corridor.

Instantly, Tom felt a warm fuzzy feeling in his head. Then it turned into a soft buzzing noise. He shook his head, trying to make the distracting sound stop, but it didn't. Then the buzzing turned into something else: a girl's voice. It whispered softly: 'Tom . . . Tom, help us!'

'Can you hear that? A voice?' Tom's eyes were wild, staring in disbelief at Eve and Clovis, who just looked blankly back at him.

'I can't hear anything, mate,' answered Clovis. 'Can you?'

Eve shrugged her shoulders and looked quizzically at Tom. 'Nothing.'

Tom let out a long breath and then whispered, 'Well, I wonder if it was Annie again? If it was her, she said my name!' He shivered with the creepiness of it all.

'I think it was Annie,' said Eve. 'You've obviously got a connection with her. Mind you, I don't think I'd fancy hearing spooky voices whispered in my ear. Are you OK?' She touched her friend's arm, he looked so worried and scared.

'I'm all right, it's just really frightening hearing voices when no one else can hear them.' Tom lifted his thumb up to his mouth, and just as he was about to start nibbling nervously at his nail, Clovis grabbed his hand and pulled it away.

'You won't have a thumb left if you keep gnawing at it. It'll be all right, Tom. I bet the spirits of Annie and Joe just want help and I think you made a connection with them earlier.'

'Yeah, maybe,' said Tom. 'I don't know why, but I feel

like I know them, understand them. I know it sounds crazy, but that's how I feel.' He shrugged his shoulders and sniffed.

Eve took his hand and squeezed it, she knew that Tom was a little more emotional at the moment, what with his mum having left. Maybe that was the reason why the ghostly children liked him. His feelings were new and raw, and their spirits were picking up on his energy. They had something in common, they both were missing their mums.

Suddenly the familiar but unnerving knocking and tapping sound could be heard. It grew louder and louder with every thud and bang. Eve, Tom and Clovis all looked to each other nervously. What was happening?

Within seconds a ball of light floated towards them from out of the dark corridor. It seemed to be getting bigger and bigger.

'Oh my God! What is that?' asked Eve, pointing at the light developing in front of them.

Boris wagged his stubby tail and barked once happily.

The light began to divide into two. Then two shapes began to emerge, one larger than the other.

'What's happening?' asked Eve.

'It's all right, Eve,' said Tom, stepping forward.

'Careful, Tom,' urged Clovis.

The shapes formed into two figures, a girl and a boy. They were slightly see-through and seemed to flicker on and off, like a TV that wasn't quite picking up a strong signal.

The ghost children were both dressed in white and looked

as though they had been swimming. Their hair was drenched, their skin white. Their long nightgowns reached to the floor, which was by now running with water.

'I hope our cameras are getting all this,' whispered Clovis through gritted teeth.

Tom, closest to the two ghosts, noticed that his feet were now submerged in a pool of water.

The girl ghost, Annie, came forward and held her hand out towards Tom; Joe, the little boy, gripped her nightgown.

Again, Tom heard the whispering of the girl's voice; it felt like a feather dancing inside his brain, an itch he couldn't scratch.

'Help us. Jack's coming for us. We want our mother.'

It was such a sad, pleading voice. Was it still just him who could hear it?

'Come on, guys, please tell me you heard that? You must have done!' He kept his voice low and didn't move a muscle, not daring to scare off the two little apparitions.

Clovis and Eve both looked at their friend in astonishment.

'No, I didn't,' replied Eve, looking astonished.

'If you can hear a voice, Tom, just go with it, don't be scared,' whispered Clovis.

Tom was positive now, he knew he was hearing little Annie's voice.

'I can definitely hear Annie's voice,' he whispered, noticing his own voice was shaking. 'She's saying that Jack is trying to get them and she wants her mum.' Tom, Eve and Clovis didn't take their eyes off the ghostly children, who hadn't moved an inch more. They looked frozen in time, trapped in a painful existence beyond any rational understanding.

The spirit of Annie looked old before its time, her small round face showed wrinkles and creases in her white papery skin. Joe sucked his thumb, keeping his little blond head down.

'We will help you, Annie, don't worry. I promise,' whispered Tom.

Annie's face lit up, but it quickly darkened once more. She whispered to Tom again, *Help your friend. Jack has gone.*'

And slowly, she and Joe began to disappear.

Tom turned quickly to the others. 'We have to help the professor,' he said with urgency. 'Annie says that Jack has gone. But the professor needs us.'

'Oh no! Is Uncle Rufus in trouble?' shouted Eve, panic rising in her throat. She didn't wait for Tom to answer but bolted through the office and up the stairs. The others were close behind.

'Be careful, Eve, wait!' shouted Clovis, but there was no stopping her.

Not checking to see if the ghost of Jack the Ripper was still present, she barrelled towards her uncle, who was lying on the floor, holding his arm.

CHAPTER 14

A Good Night's Sleep and a Terrible Deception

Uncle Rufus let Boris plant hot sticky licks all over his face and he opened his eyes slowly. He moaned out loud, his head pounding with pain. Tom, Eve and Clovis were leaning over him, Boris clearly delighted to be reunited with his master.

'We must get out,' said the professor, trying to sit up. Pain exploded up his arm and he shouted out in excruciating agony as a burning sensation seared through his skin.

'Don't worry, Uncle, it's safe now,' said Eve. 'Annie's ghost told us that Jack has gone. She said you needed help, so we rushed up here straight away. Here . . . careful.' She propped up her uncle's head gently with her arm.

Uncle Rufus felt battered and bruised, his senses slightly dulled. But his memory of what had just happened was all too clear. To top it off, his new formula hadn't worked at all. He was disappointed, exhausted and felt utterly defeated. He looked about the worried young faces and swallowed hard, feeling his tongue stick to the roof of his mouth.

'My dears, I fear I've failed again in sending Jack away,' he whispered.

'You mean you saw him, Professor?' asked Clovis, carefully helping his hero into a sitting position.

'I certainly did. Check to see if the EMF meters are still fluctuating: Jack may still be here.' Uncle Rufus looked about, worried; he didn't want the kids to come face to face with Jack's ghost.

'I did, Professor,' replied Clovis. 'First thing Tom and I did when we came upstairs, and there's no activity. The ghosts of Annie and Joe were right, Jack's gone.'

'I think . . .' said Eve. 'They're *all* gone.'

'You're right, the atmosphere has changed and it's getting a lot warmer,' said Tom.

Uncle Rufus stood up slowly, winced in pain and rolled his sleeve back. There, under Eve's torchlight, they could all see a burn mark. It was bright red and deeply impressed into Uncle Rufus's forearm.

'Bloody hell!' gasped Tom.

'Oh, Uncle, no!' cried Eve. She hugged him tight, tears sliding down her face.

'Now, now, Eve, it's all right. It will fade with time, I'm sure. It just hurts, that's all.'

'What happened?' asked Eve, sniffing.

'Annie was right. Jack did arrive, and let me tell you — he is evil. He's stronger than the last time I encountered him and threw me around like a rag doll. His spirit is certainly not to be trifled with — under no circumstances are you to be anywhere near him. With Boris's keen senses and our equipment, we have warning devices which will at least give you time to get away. For now, I think we should call it a night. I'm exhausted and as I always say, when tiredness comes, mistakes are made. We need to rethink how to deal with Jack. The technique I used tonight proved useless with him.'

Uncle Rufus switched his torch on and walked slowly over to his box of tricks. He searched around the floor with his torchlight for the two pieces of equipment that had failed him. When he found what he was looking for, he picked up the empty vial and carefully closed the hexagonal box, he put them back where they belonged, locked the lid and then placed the object inside his rucksack.

As he looked up, he saw that Clovis, Tom and Eve had been watching his every move.

'It's another invention of mine, but sadly it proved useless tonight. I need to do some more work on it,' explained Uncle Rufus. He winced in pain as his arm throbbed once more. He looked at the raw, red mark again. It was a definite branding of some kind; the shape of a figure of eight on its side with a two-lined cross jutting upwards was becoming clearer with every second.

'It looks very similar to the one that Mr Wilson has,' said Clovis, peering closely at the bright red burn.

'Have you got the pictures of it on your phone?' asked Uncle Rufus.

'Yes.'

'Good, then later, after some sleep, we can compare the two.' Uncle Rufus winced as he rolled his sleeve down. 'Well, come along then,' he said. 'Let's get home.'

Uncle Rufus carefully picked up his rucksack and patted Boris, then made for the stairs. Clovis and Eve followed.

'Do you want us to pack all the equipment away, Professor?' asked Clovis.

'No, leave everything where it is. We'll come back tomorrow and pick it all up.'

Tom remained standing in the middle of the room. He was upset, and cried out, 'Wait, Professor, what about the children? We saw them, we talked to them. We can't go, not now, and leave them with Jack. We promised we'd help them.' Tom was aware he was shouting. He couldn't leave Annie and Joe. It was he who had made the promise.

'My dear boy.' Uncle Rufus stopped at the top of the stairs. 'I want to hear all about it and I can't wait to see the footage. We *will* help them, I swear. We'll come back tomorrow, but right now we all need to rest. I feel I've been through a war.' Uncle Rufus smiled weakly and took a step to begin the descent down the wooden stairs, but was stopped by Tom's voice again.

'But, Professor, will Annie and Joe be safe? I don't want to leave here if they are in danger.' Tom's chin jutted forward, determination etched all over his face.

'I promise, Annie and Joe will be all right for the next few hours at least. Jack's spirit needs to recharge. It will be quiet in the school tonight. Trust me. All right?' Uncle Rufus smiled warmly at Tom, and then waved him over to join him.

Tom reluctantly went to Uncle Rufus where he was met with a hug and a ruffle of his unruly blond hair.

Everyone was exhausted when they arrived back at Eve's house. After reading a text from his mum reminding him to brush his teeth, Clovis slid into the spare bed and immediately fell asleep.

Eve fussed over her uncle, tending to his burn. After she had bathed and bandaged up his arm, she marched him off to bed.

Tom sat in the front room. It was dark, but he didn't want to put the light on. He couldn't stop thinking about Annie and Joe. They had been murdered by Jack the Ripper, but why? He was the most notorious serial killer of the nineteenth century. But he had killed women, not children. It didn't make sense. What upset him more was that even in death they were still running from him, still terrified. How was that possible? How was it fair?

Suddenly, Tom began to panic as he felt the rushing sensation in his head again. Then he heard it. It was her voice, Annie's voice, calling out his name.

He shot off the sofa as if he'd been electrocuted. This couldn't be happening, thought Tom. He had accepted it in the school. Hearing a ghost in your head while being in the same place was acceptable, right? But the last thing he wanted was to hear a ghostly voice when he was at home or staying with a friend. What the hell was happening to him? Terrified, Tom turned slowly around, half expecting to see Clovis or Eve hiding behind a chair. Were they pranking him? Deep down he knew not, he had definitely heard that voice before. It was so loud and frightening. What if he was losing it? What if he was going mad?

'Tom, help us!'

Tom screeched out loud and swore. His head was pulsating, the voice echoed around and around inside his brain.

Help, Tom. Help!'

Eve burst into the room suddenly and flicked a lamp on. The bright light hurt Tom's eyes.

'What the hell? . . . Tom, are you all right? What's wrong? You look petrified.' She went to him and put her arms around him. She was worried about him, they all were.

Tom surprised her by moving back and gripping her arms tightly.

'Eve, I think I'm going mad.' He stared intently at her with big, worried eyes.

'What do you mean?' asked Eve, becoming a little panicky. It was clear Tom was upset about something.

'Promise you won't laugh or think I'm crazy.'

'Don't be daft, of course not. What's the matter?' Eve took hold of Tom's hands and squeezed them.

He took a breath and decided to just tell her. 'I've just heard Annie's voice again.'

Eve's head jolted back with surprise, her eyes wide in astonishment.

'Are you sure? What did she say?'

'She said to help her. It was so clear, Eve. Is this normal? Does this mean they've followed us home again? Honestly, I'm really scared. I don't want to hear dead people's voices in my head.'

Tom was clearly distressed and upset. Eve had known him for most of her life and she knew Tom was not one for drama.

'Right, first things first,' she said. 'It's late and we're exhausted and we've had a really eventful day. We all need a good night's sleep. Let's talk to Uncle Rufus in the morning. He'll know more about this sort of stuff. But for now, let's get some sleep.'

'You're right, I know,' said Tom, relaxing a little. 'But I can't stop thinking about them. We promised to help them . . .'

'That's probably why you think you're hearing their voices. I know you're worried about them, we all are, but you need to give yourself a break. Just stop thinking about them now and think of something else. How about your next football match? Think about that, and how you're going to score a hat-trick and be Man of the Match.'

Tom smiled warmly at his friend and yawned.

'You need sleep, Tom. C'mon,' she said.

Eve tugged at Tom's hand and pulled him out of the front

room, propelling him up the stairs until they reached the landing where they said their goodnights.

Tom turned the handle of his bedroom door and began to push but stopped suddenly: he could hear the professor's voice rising in whispered annoyance in the next bedroom. He leaned closer to the professor's door and listened.

'I'm sorry, Ruthers, but I don't want to risk it. Jack's soul is so strong now, much more violent than the last time. I don't want to put the kids at risk. Yes . . . Yes, I know what I said and I stand by that. They are excellent investigators and in time will become extraordinary, but I don't think you, I or the SPI would want to jeopardise their futures. Please just let me go in and get rid of Jack first, *then* we'll see about Annie and Joe. We can't help those ghost children until we've got rid of Jack . . . No . . . no, I'm not taking Eve or the boys back there while he's still roaming about. All right? . . . Good . . . No, I know what you said about the demon hunter but just let me have one last crack at Jack before you send him in. I'm *sure* I've got the correct formula this time . . . It just wasn't strong enough today . . . He's so dangerous, Ruthers, he must be stopped. He can't escape again . . . No, I need to do this myself. I refuse for this beast to get the better of me. He did it before, well, he won't do it again, that I promise. Yes . . . I'll be careful. Thanks, Ruthers. I'll call tomorrow with an update.'

Tom couldn't believe what he had just overheard. They *weren't* going back to help Annie and Joe after all! This was awful. He had promised those two children that they would help them. The thought of them being alone in the school with the ghost of Jack the Ripper was too horrible to bear.

He tiptoed back to his door, crept inside his room and lay down wearily on his bed. He didn't know what to think. He'd have to plead with the professor in the morning. He was sure Eve and Clovis would back him up.

He placed his hands behind his head and closed his eyes, hoping that sleep would come soon. But it was no use, his mind wandered as he replayed the day's events and he hoped to God that he didn't hear any more of the ghostly voices.

He thought about his mum too, he'd hoped she would have phoned him. She'd said she would once she was settled in Leeds. He snapped his eyes opened and remembered he hadn't checked his phone since they'd got back. He leaned across to the bedside table and looked. Squinting in the brightness, he could see that he had one voicemail message. Quickly he touched his screen to play it and to his utter relief he heard his mum's voice.

'Tom, it's me. Sweetheart, I hope you're OK? I've spoken to Claudette and she says you're at Eve's. Please don't worry about me. I just needed some space from your dad, you know how he is. Everything will be all right, you'll see. I think you'll like Leeds. I'll call you again tomorrow. I love you and miss you so much. I can't wait to see you and give you a big hug. Love you . . .'

She paused and then Tom heard a terrible noise. It was

his mum crying, and then he heard her final, hiccupped words before the message ended: *'I hate being apart from you.'*

Tom stared at his phone as tears began to slide down his face. The built-up emotion of the last couple of days, which he had managed to hide from everyone, came tumbling out. He pushed his face into the pillow and sobbed silently.

They had always been close. It had been the two of them against the world, especially when Dad went off on his tour of duty in Afghanistan and came back so different. Tom hated being apart from her too. So it looked as if he and Mum would definitely be moving to Leeds, then. He tapped on the voicemail number on his phone and listened to her message again.

After he had listened another three times, he decided to call her. He didn't want to wake her, he just wanted to talk. But just as he was about to tap on her name, the terrible buzzing and pulsating in his head came back. Suddenly a whooshing feeling radiated all over his body. He tried to block the noise out, push it all away, but couldn't. Then, to his horror he heard that voice again. It was so soft.

'Tom, it's me, Annie.'

He began to panic; his breathing came in fearful gulps. What was happening to him?

'Tom, please don't leave us. He's coming to get us. Help us, please!' Annie's voice rose in pitch, higher and higher, becoming hysterical. Tom slapped both hands over his ears

and gritted his teeth, whispering over and over again, 'No, stop, stop!'

'Come and help us, Tom. Please don't leave us alone. We want our mother. We're frightened.' Annie was crying now and Tom could hear a smaller cry too, of little Joe sobbing.

Tom screamed out in his mind: *ALL RIGHT!*

He took deep slow breaths, trying to calm himself down. He knew then in an instant that he couldn't ignore the voices. He had to do something to help Annie and Joe, but what?

The others were asleep and it looked as if they weren't going to go back to the school to help the children tomorrow as promised. It was clear that the professor was very worried and didn't want them to come to any harm. But if the professor couldn't capture Jack, then what would happen to Annie and Joe? Tom knew he needed to save them without putting anyone else in harm's way.

Suddenly Annie's voice rushed back again. *'Come now, Tom, please,'* it echoed.

He realised with surprise that he was sitting up in the middle of his bed, sweating and shaking. Taking more deep breaths, he managed to calm himself down.

He lay back down, trying to sleep for what felt like hours. But it was no good. His mind kept whirring. Suddenly, a thought struck him. If he couldn't be with his own mum, then maybe he could bring Annie and Joe back to theirs. They seemed to trust him, didn't they? They obviously had a connection. Was it because they, like him, were missing their mother? Was that why they were turning to him? Tom remembered his mum's final words on the voicemail: *'I hate being apart from you.'*

Tom jumped off the bed and paced the room, back and forth. What could he do? He had to do something. A strange idea slid into his brain, he didn't like it at all and immediately blanked it out. But then like a sly snake the idea crawled back in; this time he didn't bat it away, he stopped pacing the room and stood completely still: what if he borrowed the professor's new invention, Endeavour, and took the children to the Otherside? The machine was upstairs in the professor's attic and Tom had watched how to assemble it. He knew the coordinates were already programmed in for the Veil. All he had to do was go to the school, entice Annie and Joe into the back compartment of Endeavour and then pedal like mad.

Tom nibbled on his thumbnail: should he do it? He knew it would be a treacherous thing to do, the professor would never trust him again, or worse, *speak* to him and he would definitely be thrown out of SPI. But if he was leaving London anyway, did that really matter? Surely keeping his promise was more important.

Weighing everything up, he decided in a split second that it was just something that had to be done and blow the consequences. If it meant that Annie and Joe were reunited with their mum then all the aggro would be worth it. At least *they* would be with their mother. And selfishly, he wanted the spooky whisperings of Annie and Joe to stop.

He grabbed his two pillows, plumped them up and laid them in a line down the bed then covered them with the duvet. If someone came into his room later, they would think he was still asleep. He changed back into his jeans and T-shirt, then slipped his trainers on and made his way upstairs as quickly and quietly as he could.

He opened the attic door just an inch and spied through the gap, making sure that the professor wasn't there. Thankfully, the coast seemed clear. Tiptoeing across the wooden floor, trying not to stand on any creaky floorboards, he made his way over to the suitcase. He picked it up and moved silently and shamefully back towards the door. As he passed the professor's desk, he took a pair of goggles. Carefully, he sneaked down the stairs and, once in the hallway, he grabbed his rucksack and scribbled a note for Uncle Rufus in case something went wrong. The only sounds from the otherwise silent, sleeping house were the snores and farts of Boris, who slept in the kitchen, and the soft tick-tocking of the old grandfather clock.

Opening the front door, Tom slipped out, and shut it behind him as quietly as possible. The birds were beginning their dawn chorus, although it was still dark. Tom felt slightly better knowing the daylight would soon be here. He didn't want to spend too long inside the school in the dark on his own.

He walked as quickly as he could and within minutes he was standing outside the school.

Now it looked even scarier than it had a few hours earlier. He stood on the pavement, looking through the gates. Everything was still and quiet. He had remembered the code for the main gate and door after watching the professor use them earlier. Pressing the numbers into the keypad, the gates creaked open.

Shivering in the night air, Tom moved quickly to the main door and again pressed more numbers into the keypad. Instantly a buzzer sounded and *click* . . . Good, he was in. Feeling apprehensive and vulnerable, he entered the building, but he was spurred on by the need to help the children and then get the hell out. Coming face to face with the ghost of Jack the Ripper was not on his list of things he fancied doing.

He stood in the middle of the reception area and scanned his torch around. Everything was how he remembered it. He decided to set Endeavour up in the middle of the corridor, as that seemed to be a thoroughfare for the ghost children. Hopefully they would come his way pretty soon. He set the suitcase down on its side and pressed the handle in, stepped back and after a few seconds, the suitcase began to unfold, forming itself into the unassuming wardrobe. Tom opened the doors and placed the goggles over his eyes.

Satisfied he was ready, he stood in front of Endeavour, squared his shoulders, took a huge breath for courage and began to call the ghosts of Annie and Joe.

'Annie, Joe, are you there? It's me, Tom, your friend. I've come to help you find your mother.'

BANG!

A door smashed closed. It sounded like one of the classroom doors at the end of the corridor. Tom spun round and swore under his breath. His inner voice was screaming, telling him that this was a very stupid idea and that he should run. But he pushed the thoughts away. The eerie sound of little feet running came rushing towards him.

'Hello, is that you? Annie, Joe?'

He could hear a strange whooshing noise, and for a second he wondered what it was. To his relief he realised that it was his own blood rushing through his head. Every part of his being was telling him to run and never come back, but he knew he couldn't, he knew that he wouldn't leave the ghost children alone and scared. He understood their need to be with their mum.

All of a sudden, he heard a giggle. Whether it was Joe or Annie, he couldn't tell, but it was a sure sign that the children were close by. Then came a terrible noise, a deep wail followed by crying.

Tom looking nervously around him. 'Is that you? Annie? Joe?' He stood shaking, turning slowly in a circle, his torchlight shuddering past the drawings and paintings on the walls. Close to his ear, he felt an icy-cold blast then the whispered word, *'Yes.'*

'Arghh!' Tom jumped again, then realised quickly that he had to get a grip. He had come here on his own to do something. He must get on with it.

'Right,' he said, swallowing his nerves. 'I'm going to start this machine.' He pointed at Endeavour, imagining that Annie and Joe were watching him. 'If you want to be with your mother, then when you see a bright light, you must get inside.' He pulled down on the chain and watched as the see-through door at the back opened. He then went to the rear of the wardrobe and pointing at the compartment, he said: 'You must come in this way and stay inside until I tell you to get out. Do you understand, Annie? Do you trust me?'

Again, another little icy whisper fluttered into Tom's ear. *Yes.*

Tom walked around to the front of the wardrobe and jumped onto the unicycle, then he closed the wardrobe door.

Gosh, it was a tight squeeze. He peered through his goggles, which were beginning to fog up, and checked on the computer screen that the coordinates were there. A long line of numbers and letters blinked at him. He knew that once he began to ride, he would be at the machine's mercy.

'Right, here we go then.' He began to pedal, slowly at first, the little kites moving around on the track, making a clacking and humming noise. When Tom was at full speed, sparks spat and sizzled and slowly the little dark space began to get brighter. Now the noise was terrific, and a whirring sounded all around him. Soon the brightness became incredibly intense. He kept looking through his goggles at the space he had asked Annie and Joe to enter, and to his delight he could just make out through the blaze of powerful light the shadows of two figures walking towards Endeavour. One hoot from the cuckoo clock signalled that the correct atmosphere had been reached so Tom pulled down on the chain and watched as the door to the compartment at the back opened. He kept pedalling furiously. Looking again, he saw with joy that Annie and Joe were now inside the small space, so pulling again on the chain, he closed the doors and shouted over the tremendous din.

'It's all right, I'm taking you to see your mum, don't be frightened.'

He couldn't see the children now but he knew they were there. What with the bright light and steamed-up goggles, it was impossible to see anything at all. His legs were aching, the sound was incredible, it reminded Tom of an old-fashioned steam train thundering through a tunnel. He wondered how much longer he had to keep going. His body was screaming to stop and just as he was about to slow down, he heard the terrific and very satisfying sound of the cuckoo warbling three times. It was music to his ears.

They had arrived, they had reached the entrance to the Otherside. He stopped pedalling, the light inside the compartment began to fade and the steam diminished quickly. He took off the goggles and looked through the transparent partition. To his astonishment Annie and Joe were both standing there with their little palms pressed against the see-through wall, smiling up at him. They looked so happy, elated, in fact. Annie smiled shyly and Joe waved happily, jumping up and down. After the cuckoo had signalled, Tom pulled on the chain and watched as the children walked out into a beautiful hue of light.

'Wait!' shouted Tom, and without thinking he jumped down off the unicycle and opened the doors of Endeavour. He stopped suddenly in his tracks, for all around him was nothing but a beautiful, vibrant radiance. It was the most magnificent light he had ever seen and the feeling in his stomach was a strange mix of pure contentment and, yes . . . *love*.

He felt so light, he looked down at his hands and noticed they were slightly translucent. Odd!

He went round to the back of Endeavour and realised he wasn't walking, but gliding. His body felt so featherlike, so free. Wisps of colour were now floating about him, each one like a tiny breath of the freshest air he had ever known. Tom could make out the shapes of Annie and Joe just in front of him, and they turned around to look at him with a smile.

CHAPTER 15

Some Analysis and a Missing Tom

Clovis was woken by a light tap on the bedroom door.

Uncle Rufus popped his head through: 'Clovis, wake up! Come and see what I've discovered.' Clovis sprang out of bed and got dressed quickly. As he ran along the landing, he nearly crashed into Eve, who was obviously still trying to come round. Her dressing gown dragged on the floor, and she scratched her head and yawned loudly.

'What's the rush? Bloody hell, Uncle, it's too early,' Eve moaned away as she slowly made her way up the stairs towards Uncle Rufus's attic. Clovis was standing outside the door and waved at her to hurry up. They knocked and waited.

'Yes, yes. Come in!' called Uncle Rufus.

Eve and Clovis poked their heads round the door and looked in on a scene that would have been befitting of a theatrical performance of *Frankenstein*.

Uncle Rufus was standing behind his large desk, which had been transformed into a chemistry bench. Test tubes, Bunsen burners and all manner of strange coloured liquids were bubbling away.

'Well, someone's been busy,' said Eve under her breath.

'Where's Tom?' asked Clovis, yawning.

'Oh, I didn't want to wake him. I called him, but he was dead to the world so I thought we should let him sleep. I think the poor chap deserves a lie-in with everything that's going on, you know . . . with his mum and dad. Now, come here, you two, and take a look at these water samples.'

Uncle Rufus gestured to a microscope sitting centre stage on his desk.

'If you look through the microscope, you'll see I've placed a slide with a drop of water on it. Eve, come and have a look and tell me what you see.'

She did as he asked and quickly whipped her head back in disgust. 'Ergh! That's horrible, there's some creatures and worms in it. Is that the water from the footprints we took?'

Clovis leaned in and looked through the microscope. 'I'm taking a guess and thinking that it is, Professor. It looks like contaminated water.'

'What you are looking at is unfiltered water from our own taps, and as you can see, it's quite lively.'

Uncle Rufus got the reaction he expected.

'Oh my God! That can't be right. We drink that stuff?' said Eve, clearly disgusted.

Uncle Rufus was laughing. 'And that, my dear girl, is *clean*. The microbes you are seeing there are mostly good bacteria — think what the drinking water must be like in poorer countries.'

'So, what does the footprint water look like?' asked Clovis.

'Ah, ah, just wait.' Uncle Rufus was enjoying himself. He placed another slide onto the stand of the microscope and invited Clovis to look.

'Wow! Now that looks like a jungle,' laughed Clovis.

'Let me see,' said Eve, pushing Clovis out of the way. She took a quick peek, squealed and then swore.

'Now we know where Mr Pig is getting some of his choice new words from. Less of that, dear girl.'

'Sorry, Uncle, but that is *gross*,' she said, backing away from the microscope.

'That is from the oldest and dirtiest water supply I could find. It's from the well at the bottom of the garden. I thought that could be the closest to the age and state of the footprint water . . . but it doesn't match. This is somewhat extraordinary. Take a look at the water from the footprints.' Uncle Rufus placed a third slide under the microscope and invited Clovis to take another look.

Clovis didn't say anything, he brought his head back in confusion, looked at Uncle Rufus, then at Eve and then looked again.

'Well?' asked Eve, getting impatient. 'Let me have a go.' She scrunched her eyes up and gazed at the slide. 'There's nothing there,' she said, sounding rather disappointed.

'Precisely,' laughed Uncle Rufus.

'What does that mean, Professor?' asked Clovis.

'Well, I tested our tap water during many runs with Endeavour to the Otherside, and discovered that the microbes in the water survived while inside the compartment. Nothing altered whatsoever. But this water sample from the school has nothing, no cells, microbes or living bacteria in the water, not a thing!'

'I don't get it,' said Eve, looking confused.

'It means,' continued Uncle Rufus, 'that no living matter can survive in the Veil, the Otherside, or indeed any other dimension. It makes me realise the importance of the sealed compartment at the front of Endeavour. I must do more testing to see how long before matter expires outside of the machine when it reaches the Veil. In conclusion, the physical self would cease to exist. How long that would take, I've yet to discover, but the soul, the spirit, would travel on.' Uncle Rufus began to scribble equations and diagrams on his small notebook.

'So, what you're saying is a human body would die if transported to any other plane or dimension?' said Eve.

'Exactly! And this water proves to me that it did indeed come from the ghost children. Any being that is not of the earthly plane, has no human make-up, no cells, is just pure energy. Even in between dimensions there is no human living matter. Fascinating.' Uncle Rufus whispered the word more to himself than to Clovis and Eve.

Eve noticed the creepy-looking doll that Mr Wilson had given them was lying on the desk. It looked so strange and out of place. It had helped them get good results last night though, as Annie had tapped out that it was hers.

'What about her?' She placed the doll on the desk next to the microscope. 'Any luck?'

'Well, the only thing that anyone can really do is date it, and for that we need to look closely at the body,' said Uncle Rufus. He took an enormous magnifying glass and began to inspect the doll's small torso.

'Mmm, mmm,' Uncle Rufus muttered to himself as he searched for a clue. Eve and Clovis watched, fascinated.

'It has a wax head . . . one glass eye is missing, not too much damage, which is amazing considering its time under the ground. Cloth body, wax hands and legs but, aha! Yes . . . here, look, can you see the small stamp on the back of her thigh?'

Clovis and Eve leaned in close to get a better look. The stamp was tiny, but through the magnifying glass they could clearly read where and by whom it had been made.

Joseph Evans and Sons
Manufacturers and importers
114 - 116 Newgate St
London E.C.

'Clovis, type that into the search engine and find out when they were making dolls,' instructed Uncle Rufus.

Clovis tapped away while Eve looked over his shoulder.

'There,' she said, pointing at the screen. 'It says the company made dolls from eighteen sixty-eight to eighty-one.

So, if Jack was killing in eighteen eighty-eight, that means the doll could very well have belonged to Annie.'

'She did tap out on the board that she was killed "here".' Clovis used his fingers to emphasise quotation marks. 'With the doll being found in the school's grounds, that seems to suggest that the children *were* murdered by Jack, on the land where the school now stands?'

'Why is this the first time we've ever heard of it? Wouldn't it be part of Jack's history of killing?' asked Eve. 'Unless the police just missed it or . . .'

'Covered it up?' added Clovis.

'It's all very odd. I wonder what Tom thinks. I'll go and wake him. He'll love all this,' said Eve. She dashed out of the room and down the stairs, then knocked lightly on Tom's door.

'Oi! Wake up, you lazy sod!'

After getting no reply she knocked again.

'Come on, lazy bones, it's time to get up.' Still nothing. That's odd, thought Eve. Tom was usually quite a light sleeper.

'I'm coming in,' she warned, opening the door.

The room was still dark apart from some light that crept around the sides of the heavy dark curtains. Through the dimness Eve could just make out the shape of Tom underneath the duvet. Grinning mischievously, she jumped onto the bed.

'Aha! Get up!' she cried in delight.

He didn't move. 'Tom?' Eve pulled back the cover, revealing two pillows positioned in a line. 'What the . . . ?' Eve bolted out of the door and ran downstairs. Was Tom pranking her?

Maybe he was in the kitchen making breakfast? She looked in the room but nothing.

Boris snuffled out of his basket, yawned, farted and then slunk back off again into his warm pit.

Eve went into the front room. Mr Pig greeted her from inside his cage. Eve opened it up and let the parrot out.

'Tom's gone! Arse!' squawked the bird. Eve ran back into the hallway and noticed a piece of folded paper on the side table. She opened it and read quickly.

Dear all,

Don't get mad but I couldn't sleep knowing Annie and Joe were frightened. They need to be with their mum and I know what that feels like. I've gone back to the school to help them. I've taken Endeavour. I'm so sorry, Professor. Please forgive me and don't worry.

Love Tom x

'Oh my God! Tom, you bloody idiot.' Eve ran her fingers through her messed-up morning hair then rushed upstairs shouting at the top of her voice.

'Uncle . . . Clovis!'

They heard her and came running.

'What on earth's the matter?' asked Uncle Rufus, alarmed at the distress in her voice.

Eve ran up the stairs waving Tom's note in the air. 'It's Tom, he's gone back to the school to save the children,' she said breathlessly.

'He's done what?!' yelled Uncle Rufus. His face aged in a second, all the colour draining from it. Fear and a sudden sickness prickled through his body. Why had the boy done this? He knew Tom was going through an emotional time at the moment, but to sneak off and possibly put himself in danger was just foolish. 'Right . . . get dressed, Eve, come on, Clovis,' said Uncle Rufus, grabbing his rucksack and making for the stairs.

'But, Uncle, there's more,' whispered Eve. 'He's taken Endeavour.'

'But that's insane!' cried Clovis.

Uncle Rufus was furious and his face went a bright shade of red. How could Tom have done something so utterly stupid? The professor wasn't bothered about his machine, he was worried for the boy. Tom didn't know how to use it properly and Endeavour was nowhere near ready yet. If anything happened to him, he'd never forgive himself.

CHAPTER 16

The Ghost of Elizabeth Tells All

Within minutes, Clovis, Uncle Rufus, Boris and Eve were all in the car and speeding through the streets of Whitechapel. Uncle Rufus screeched the little Mini to a stop outside the school. They ran up to the gate, tapped in the code and watched with frustration as the gates ever so slowly began to open. As soon as they were wide enough for them to fit through, they dashed to the entrance.

Once inside, Uncle Rufus locked the door from the inside. Through the window he caught sight of a man watching them suspiciously between the railings of the gates. He couldn't see his face because his collar was pulled up. Uncle Rufus stared, his eyes following the man until he walked out of sight.

'What are you doing, Uncle Rufus? Come on!' urged Eve.

'Tom!' Clovis shouted out. 'Where are you?'

'Quick, start searching, he can't be far,' said Uncle Rufus, sprinting up the corridor. 'Clovis, take Eve and search upstairs,' he shouted over his shoulder.

Eve, Clovis and Boris ran up to the attic. They looked

behind boxes and in dark corners, but found nothing. Everyone met back in the corridor.

'There's no sign of him,' said Eve, starting to get upset.

'Maybe he's been and gone,' said Clovis.

'Look . . .' Uncle Rufus pointed to a space on the floor. Black soot marks formed the shape of a large rectangle.

'He's definitely been here, and by the looks of it he's inside Endeavour.' Uncle Rufus's expression was a mixture of anger, frustration and worry.

'Oh no! Where has he gone, Professor?' asked Clovis, looking very worried.

'That, my dear boy, I do not know.'

Tom couldn't believe the place Endeavour had brought him to. It felt so comfortable, so *right*. He couldn't see anything much, just beautiful clouds and colourful mists. Annie and Joe were thrilled to have their new friend with them and clasped his hands in theirs. For a moment everything seemed perfect, no worries or cares, nothing to be frightened of.

Something in the distance suddenly caught the children's attention. Tom followed their gaze and noticed something shimmering in the misty void. A fluid movement of colourful clouds swirled about into an elongated column and began to form the outline of a misty white figure. An intense feeling of pure joy and happiness swept over Tom's body as he watched the figure glide towards them. No one was frightened, they knew whatever was approaching wasn't anything to be fearful of, but who was it?

Tom knew within seconds because Annie and Joe let out squeals of delight. He watched as they ran towards the shimmering white outline. The figure kneeled down to the two children. Her form became clearer and Tom witnessed something incredibly moving. The iridescent spirit of a pretty young woman pulled Annie and Joe into her arms and began to silently cry and sob. She folded her arms tightly around the two children and held them close to her as she rocked them back and forth. She kissed their eyes, their hair and their little faces. Annie and Joe held on tight for fear of being ripped away again. But this time, there was no need to fear. They were reunited and safe and could spend the rest of eternity happily together with their mother.

Suddenly more white, wispy figures began to emerge from the colourful mist. As the shadows came closer, Tom sucked in his breath and gulped it down. The ethereal figures stopped a safe distance away from Tom and all looked on at the wonderful scene unfolding before them, obviously delighted at the emotional reunion. Then the mother floated towards Tom, the children still held close in her arms. She smiled radiantly and leaned forward and kissed Tom's cheek. He felt the slightest warm flutter like a butterfly's wing touching his skin.

The strange buzzing and fizzing phenomenon started to

rush around Tom's head again. He knew now what this meant and waited for Annie's voice to echo inside his mind, but this time it wasn't Annie he heard, it was her mother.

'Hello, Tom. I'm Lucy Abbot, Annie and Joe's mother. Thank you so much for bringing them back to me. I've been trying for so long to reach them but they have been distracted by fear and terror of that *creature*.'

'But what happened? How did Jack get your children?' Tom found that no words left his lips but they emanated from his mind. Oh God, he was mind reading! Stunned at this strange way of communicating, he looked on as Annie stroked her mother's face and Joe snuggled further into her embrace. Tom noticed that the two children's appearances had changed. Gone were the frightening apparitions of two wet, white-faced ghosts, now they looked like happy, rosy-cheeked children. Satisfied and happy that he was back in his mother's arms, little Joe began to suck his thumb, and his eyes slowly closed. A peaceful sleep had come at last.

Lucy stared at Tom, her face serious and stern, her startling blue eyes piercing straight into his. Tom leaned back, not quite liking this change in her persona. Was she going to harm him?

'The children were asleep in bed, as was I,' she said. 'He came into my house and murdered me in my bed. When Annie and Joe disturbed him, and he knew they could identify him, he took them and drowned them.'

Tom gasped and looked at the three of them. He was

pleased he had helped them, even though he knew it could possibly have cost him his friendship with Clovis and Eve and the professor's trust.

His thoughts were interrupted as another woman glided towards him. Her face was smooth as stone, her smile kind and serene. She wore a long white dress and her hair was flowing and silken.

Instantly the familiar feeling of buzzing whizzed around his head again. He was beginning to get used to this odd sensation. He wondered who this woman was, who seemed to want to communicate with him.

'I'm Elizabeth, I was one of Jack's victims too.' Her voice swirled about in his head.

'Oh, I'm sorry.' Tom instantly felt stupid at his reaction, but he honestly didn't know what else to say or think.

'It's all right, Tom, I'm happy now, so you don't have to feel sorry for me. I'm here with the others to help *you*.' Elizabeth turned around and gestured with her hand, introducing a crowd of about ten other women, who were now gliding further forward.

Tom could feel his body tensing up, he wasn't sure what to expect.

Elizabeth came closer to him, her face only inches away.

'You must relax, Tom, you've been given a gift, a precious gift. Few from the plane of the living can communicate with those from the Otherside. I'm going to tell you the story of how we came to be here. Close your eyes.'

Elizabeth's voice reverberated through his head. As she spoke, pictures played out in his mind.

'I was walking down Berner Street on my way home from work. It was dark and cold, so I walked quickly. I noticed that across the way, a well-dressed gentleman was talking to someone in a hushed, angry voice. It was unusual to see a posh one up that way. Then I noticed his bag, it looked like a doctor's bag, so I assumed he must be a doctor on his rounds.'

Tom could see in the flickering images the man Elizabeth was describing. Part of him wanted to run away and part of him knew he had to stay, knew he had to see what happened to this woman and Annie and Joe. Tom gritted his teeth and forced himself to listen as Elizabeth continued to recount her terrible story.

'I was going to walk past the gentleman but then I saw something very strange. Two little children were fighting with him. They were crying and trying desperately to get away. I wasn't having that so I ran over to the man and said, "Oi, you there, those nippers don't seem to like you very much. Leave them alone!" When the man's head snapped round and stared at me, I knew I was in trouble. His face was like something dragged up from the very bowels of Hell itself. In that moment, Tom, I knew he was going to kill me; I just had a feeling in the pit of my stomach.

'I tried to turn and run,' continued Elizabeth, her voice rising in volume and fear, 'but before I could make a break for it, he was on me. The kiddies were crying, too scared to move. I tried to reach for one of them but it was no use, the only thing I managed to grab was the little girl's doll. The next thing I felt was a warm, sharp sensation around my throat. I was so shocked because I looked down and saw I was covered in a hot, red sticky liquid. When I realised it was my own blood and that he had cut me, all I could do was scream, but no noise came out of my mouth. The only sound I could produce was a bubbling and choking noise, a strange sound that I'll never forget. Then suddenly to my horror I saw myself from above. I was floating above my own dying body! I tried to call for help but of course no one could hear me. Then I watched on, helpless, as he plunged the little kiddies into a horse's drinking trough. He was drowning the poor little mites! They fought, mind, they kicked and tried to escape but they weren't strong enough for the likes of him. That was the last I saw of the children until now, as my ancestors came to get me and I was taken up into the Veil.

Tom slowly opened his eyes. The scenes he had just witnessed in his mind made him feel sick to his stomach. Swiftly Elizabeth and all the rest of the ghostly women encircled him and instantly Tom began to feel a wonderful pulsing sensation.

'Now you know what happened to me and those poor innocent children. All these women were murdered by that evil monster.'

Elizabeth continued to talk, all the while never opening her mouth to speak. 'The police at the time thought he had murdered five women but as you can see, he killed a lot more than that. Since all our deaths we've found each other and learned more about Jack. This is in the hope that we can give some information to the living to help in the final destruction of his soul. We know now that the authorities covered up the murders of Annie and Joe. If the public had heard that children were being killed, the city would have rioted. The government didn't want the public to take matters into their own hands, it was bad enough as it was, with the Ripper on the loose killing women, but children! No . . . the public wouldn't stand for that. No one felt safe and the government was under pressure to find the murderer and wrap up the case. As you know, he never was caught. Now Jack the Ripper must be stopped, once and for all, so that he can no longer terrorise the living or the dead. The professor, you, and your friends are the only ones who can help. Oh . . . my dear Tom, don't look so upset, as you can see, we are all very much at peace now. We will help the professor when the time comes, but you must hurry back to the living plane now, too much time here, and you too will pass over.'

'You mean I'll die?' Tom gasped. Suddenly the professor's warning of 'Do not leave Endeavour!' came rushing back. Oh God! What had he done? He didn't want to die, not yet, he wasn't ready. He had too much living to do.

He ran over to Endeavour, jumped inside and quickly shut the doors behind him. As he began pedalling, Tom noticed his hands seemed to be becoming *more* translucent.

Oh God, he thought. *Please get me back. I don't want to die.*

He rode faster, sparks of electricity beginning to fly all around him, and slowly, to his relief, the gentle humming sound pulsated from the machine. He pushed on and pumped his legs harder, but looking down, he saw to his horror that his feet were beginning to disappear!

Suddenly he felt very weak and saw that the handle bar was becoming blurred. Slowly, he felt his body slumping forward on the unicycle. His mind was wide awake but bizarrely he couldn't get his physical body to work. He started to panic. What was happening to him? What an idiot he had been, he should have paid more attention to what the professor said. He tried to calm down, took a deep breath and instantly felt heavy and tired again.

Suddenly he heard a voice. Was it a dream? Or his imagination?

There it was again. Tom was now slumped on the floor of the compartment and all his muscles seemed to have melted away. He felt so warm, so comfortable, but his body was disappearing. He knew that soon he would be no more. Surprisingly it didn't bother him. He liked this warm feeling, he liked it very much.

Then somewhere in the back of his mind he heard Eve

calling him. She sounded upset. Did she need his help? Her voice jolted him back to reality, bringing him round. He needed to get back to his friends. He remembered where he was, the realisation of what was happening to him was flooding through his body. The pull of Eve, Clovis and the professor was like a jolt of electricity, galvanising him. He didn't want to die, no way. He was going to get Endeavour back, if it was indeed the last thing he ever did. He gulped in as much air as possible and began to shout out, over and over again, 'Help me!'

They would hear him, wouldn't they? He knew he had managed to travel some distance but he could hear Eve. His friends would save him, they had to.

Pulling every ounce of energy he had left in his feeble and weak body he stood up slowly and began to cry out in the vain hope that he would make contact with Eve.

'Please!' he cried. 'Help me!'

He paused and listened for her voice . . . nothing. He was standing facing the wardrobe doors, but he daren't open them. What had he done? It seemed they couldn't hear him.

Panic rushed through him again, he needed to get home, wanted to see his friends. He slammed his fists against Endeavour's doors in a temper.

What was that? Tom heard a noise in the distance. It wasn't a voice, it was a *bark*. Boris! Could they really be here?

He banged his fists on the doors and began to shout, over and over again: 'Help me, it's Tom!'

Everyone stood completely still, waiting to hear something, anything. They hadn't moved from their initial spot in the school corridor. Uncle Rufus was convinced that Tom and Endeavour would reappear in the same place it had left from. He stood in the centre of the scorched rectangle, praying to any god that would listen to bring his young friend home.

'Tom, if you don't answer me now, I will never speak to you again. Do you hear me?' Eve was shouting, her anger exploding and echoing around the school. She had to find him, *had* to get her best friend back.

Clovis and Uncle Rufus kept looking up, as if by some miracle Endeavour would reappear from the heavens. Then suddenly Boris made everyone jump as he barked loudly at the ceiling. Something *was* there. What was that noise?

'It sounds like a voice,' said Clovis, whipping his head around, trying to find the source.

'Shush,' commanded Uncle Rufus.

Everyone stood completely still and to their horror, they heard a gurgled echoing voice. It whipped around them in a circle, calling out over and over again, getting louder each time. *'Help me!'*

A gust of wind blew down the corridor, slamming doors

in its wake, ripping displays of children's work from the walls. Eve, Clovis and Uncle Rufus felt the force of it roar through their bodies. They held onto each other's hands, not quite sure what was happening.

Then a terrifying sound began to escape from the building itself, a deep, thudding noise pulsating from the concrete. It sounded to Eve as if someone were trying to punch through something to escape.

'What is it, Uncle? Is it Jack?' screamed Eve, placing her hands over her ears. She was petrified. Clovis and Uncle Rufus grabbed her and pulled her closer to them.

'No, it's not him,' shouted Uncle Rufus, looking very worried.

'Help me,' echoed the voice again. The sound thundered and raged around the corridor like a small tornado. But the voice was unrecognisable.

Eve shouted out, she clenched her fists into balls, her fingernails cutting into her bunched-up palms. 'Who is this?'

Where was Tom? Had Jack taken him? The noise was so loud, tumbling around and around in a circle. But then the voice came buffeting back. Loud and clear, the windows vibrated with the strength of it. 'It's me, it's Tom!'

CHAPTER 17

Bringing the Boy Back

'Right!' shouted Uncle Rufus. 'Stand back!' He pulled Eve, Clovis and Boris to the side of the corridor, making sure the space marked by the rectangular soot marks was clear. Then he shouted. 'Tom, if you can hear me, you must press the red emergency button on the computer keyboard. It will bring you back.' Uncle Rufus fought to be heard over the din of the wind that was still whipping around them.

'Where is he, Uncle?' shouted Eve.

'He's trapped in the gateway to another plane, I think.' The little tornado began to ease but Tom's voice could no longer be heard.

'If he's heard me, he should be coming back any second now,' said Uncle Rufus, looking at his watch hopefully.

In the distance the familiar sound of humming and sparking could be heard, then a cloud of brilliant white light rumbled through the corridor, sparks of electricity flying about in every direction, reminding Clovis of sparklers on Bonfire Night. Finally, the fog of light and electricity died away to reveal an old plain-looking wooden wardrobe. It had landed in exactly the same place it had left.

Eve, Clovis and Uncle Rufus rushed to open its doors. Tom was on the floor, curled up in a ball.

'Oh, Tom! Tom!' cried Eve. She picked his head up and kissed his cheek.

'Is he all right, Professor?' asked Clovis.

Uncle Rufus tapped Tom's face gently: 'Tom, can you hear me?'

Tom moaned and opened his eyes slowly. 'Am I alive?'

Everyone let out a huge sigh of relief. 'Yes, you certainly are,' said Uncle Rufus. 'And you've got a lot of explaining to do.'

Tom sat up and nursed his pounding head. 'I'm so, so, sorry, Professor.'

'Never mind that for now, you're safe, and that's all that matters, Tom. Now what the hell happened?' said Uncle Rufus.

'Did you manage to help Annie and Joe?' whispered Eve.

'Yes, they're safe and with their mum now and ... Professor, I met *all* the victims of Jack, they're going to help us and Elizabeth, she's one of his victims, she was so ...' Tom's voice began to fade, he yawned and slowly shut his eyes.

They could get no more sense out of him. 'He's exhausted,' said Uncle Rufus. 'That's a normal reaction given where he's travelled to. We must let him rest.'

Uncle Rufus decided that they should help him to the car. Eve followed and watched as Uncle Rufus told Boris to 'Guard', wound the window down and left Tom fast asleep, protected by a dribbling Boris.

Eve and Clovis laughed. 'He won't be happy when he wakes up, not with all that dog saliva down his face,' chuckled Clovis.

'He's not going to be happy when I've finished with him either,' warned Uncle Rufus.

His face looked grim as he walked back towards the school. Eve and Clovis could hear him muttering to himself. 'Time is of the essence, I *must* hurry. Jack will hopefully still be in the atmosphere. Now is the moment to strike!'

They followed him back into the school and watched as he folded Endeavour smoothly back into its unassuming guise of a large suitcase.

Eve could tell her uncle wasn't happy; he was agitated, angry, almost. She watched as he twitched and moved about in a brusque manner, busying himself with his gadgets, folding leads and checking the cameras. She leaned in close to Clovis and whispered, 'I think Tom has ruined it for us. You know what Uncle's like. I'd say he's a bit more than angry.'

Clovis put his arm around Eve's shoulders.

'It will all be fine, you'll see. What Tom did was stupid but his heart is always in the right place. You know that, and I think the professor knows that too.'

'Yeah, you're right. We'll just have to work doubly hard

on gaining Unc's trust again. I'm just glad Tom's OK.' They both walked quietly up behind Uncle Rufus. Clovis picked up the professor's rucksack and held it out to him.

'It's all right, Clovis. I can take that.'

Clovis handed it over to the outstretched hand. 'Are you all right, Professor?'

'I'm fine,' he replied tersely.

'Well, clearly you're not. Is there anything we can do?' asked Eve, hating the strange energy that her uncle was exuding.

'Yes, just stay outside and no matter what you hear, don't, and I repeat *don't*, come up to the loft.' He looked down at his brown leather shoes and bit his bottom lip. 'If I'm not back in half an hour then I want you to take Tom and Boris home and call the inspector. She'll know what to do.'

Eve gasped and flung her arms around her uncle's neck. 'Please don't go up there alone. Let's wait for help. Maybe the inspector . . .'

Uncle Rufus stopped Eve's emotional plea by putting his hand up, and surprised them both as his voice quavered a little: 'Tom could have *died*. I was right when I said this was too much for you. This isn't a case for kids, it's too sensitive. I said at the beginning spirits of children can be difficult to deal with emotionally and I should have known that Tom wasn't in the right place mentally to deal with such matters. He's going through a lot right now. I'm a fool for allowing you all to be involved. What was I thinking?' Uncle Rufus shook his head with the frustration of it all. 'I couldn't live with myself if anything happened to any of you. So please, do as I ask and stay here.' Uncle Rufus kissed Eve's cheek and patted Clovis's back. 'I won't be long.' He slung his rucksack over his shoulder, picked up the suitcase, and went through the door that led upstairs.

'He's mad! He can't tackle Jack on his own. He said himself that he's got a lot stronger.'

'He'll be all right, he knows what he's doing, Eve, you'll see.' Eve understood that Clovis was trying to make her feel better but they both knew no reassuring words would ever help that feeling of fear that was now sliding about in their stomachs.

Up in the loft, Uncle Rufus set the suitcase down in the middle of the floor, pressed on the handle and stood back. The machine began to take shape, for what Uncle Rufus hoped was the very last time that day. He anticipated that if it were still here, the ghost of Jack the Ripper would be enticed by Endeavour's bright light. It was much more powerful than anything he had created before, so he hoped it would work. Now he knew just how strong this ghost was, he wondered if Endeavour could handle it. One thing he did know thanks to Tom was that the machine *was* successful in transporting spirits. The young lad had managed to travel to the Otherside and reunite the two ghost children with their mother. He had also managed to get back home in one piece. If the invention held out, and managed to trap Jack and send him into the Abyss, then it would be a huge relief, not just for Rufus and SPI but for the whole world. Admittedly the thought of travelling to the dark realms with the ghost of Jack the Ripper on board was something he didn't relish, but he knew he had no choice. Time was running out and he just knew it wouldn't be long until Jack struck again. Now that Tom had taken the children away from him, Jack would be on the warpath, hunting for his next victim. Time was short, he had to act now.

Uncle Rufus brought his shoulders back and stretched his arms out in front of him. Lacing his fingers together, he cracked his knuckles, then moved his head from side to side, unlocking the tense muscles in his neck. He felt like a boxing champion about to undertake the biggest fight of his life. He would do his damnedest to deliver the evil spirit to its rightful place. Jack the Ripper had to go and he was the one to do it. Uncle Rufus pushed all negative thoughts to the back of his mind and whispered, imagining his beautiful wife Jess, watching him from above, 'Please keep me safe if you can, my darling.'

Exhaling a long deep breath, he opened the doors, climbed up onto the seat of the cycle and shut himself inside. He placed the goggles over his eyes but before he even started to pedal an intense pain shot through his arm.

Pushing up his shirt sleeve, he noticed his arm seemed to

be pulsating. The deep red sore throbbed and seared. Biting down on his lip, Uncle Rufus pushed on. He had to banish this evil spirit once and for all and now was the time to do it. Endeavour hummed, intense light blazed in and around the small space. The electricity spat and sparked as he rode hard.

Looking through the sealed compartment, he could just make out the outline of something. He squinted, hoping to make his eyes see clearer. Somebody was there; he hoped it was Jack. The cuckoo clock called once, signalling that Endeavour had attracted a ghost and the atmosphere was ready. Uncle Rufus pulled down on the chain and immediately the transparent door sprung open.

A dark shadow slithered inside the compartment and instantly Uncle Rufus pulled the chain again, closing the door, and sealing in the spirit he hoped was Jack.

Uncle Rufus pressed in some new coordinates. Those were to the one place no one wanted to go. The Abyss. The mere mention of the name made the bravest person quiver in fear. But he was taking the ghost of Jack the Ripper there for good this time and once at the gateway his ghost would be dealt with in the way he deserved.

Uncle Rufus daren't look over into the compartment. He feared if he did, he would die of fright. He was on his own, travelling through multiple dimensions with an evil entity on board. He shook his head as he pedalled and whispered to himself, 'I must be mad.'

But he knew why he was doing it and he couldn't stop now. Uncle Rufus was ridding the world and the other planes of existence of the vilest monster. This ghost had evaded him before; he wasn't about to let him get away again.

Suddenly, with no warning, Endeavour banged and crashed about, as if it were rolling over a pot-holed road at high speed. Uncle Rufus held on for dear life. What was happening? He dared himself to take a look at the ghost through the sparks and smoke and saw to his terror the apparition of Jack was *laughing* at him. The professor's arm began to sizzle and blister and he screamed out loud, the intensity of pain was too much to bear.

With shock, he realised that Endeavour had stopped, the computer screen flashing the word: *Error*.

'Oh no, this can't be happening,' said Uncle Rufus, beginning to fluster. He started typing in various codes, hitting buttons, but the computer kept flashing back the terrible word, *Error*.

The ghost of Jack the Ripper pressed the side of his ravaged, scarred face up to the partition, and slowly grinned, his teeth pointed and yellow, his raging red eyes blazing in triumph.

To his horror Uncle Rufus realised the ghost had done this. He had stopped the machine! Uncle Rufus knew he would have to override Endeavour's programming, and he hit the *HOME* button. Maybe, thought the professor, once back at the school, he could hold Jack in the compartment while he sent for back-up. He certainly couldn't stay here, suspended between the planes. He didn't know what could happen.

Endeavour went into autopilot and Uncle Rufus flopped forward on the cycle, his energy gone, his arm burning again. He was in excruciating agony and he screamed out once more in pain and frustration.

Eve and Clovis were sitting outside on the school step. The sun had begun to break through the morning haze. They both sat nervously, wondering what was happening inside the building. Suddenly they heard a terrible noise. Was that Uncle Rufus screaming? They turned to each other, eyes wide, fear barrelling through them.

'We've got to go in there,' said Eve, starting to get up.

Clovis grabbed her arm to stop her. 'He told us no matter what, that we were to stay outside.'

'No, Clovis!' Eve pulled away and stood up. 'I can't stand by and hear a noise like that and do *nothing*! He obviously needs us. I don't care what he said, I'm going in.' She made a start for the door. This time, Clovis didn't try to stop her. They ran into the little office, through the door and up the stairs.

They discovered Endeavour surrounded by a fine white fog. Clovis and Eve grabbed the doorknobs and pulled open the wardrobe, where they found Uncle Rufus slumped over the handlebar, his goggles slipped down, making his face seem uneven, tortured, almost.

Smoke billowed and swirled around the inside of the machine. The back of Endeavour was shrouded in a thick fug. A mixture of vile colours rolled around together, then to Eve and Clovis's horror, they both saw what looked like hundreds of black winged insects swarming inside the compartment.

'Uncle!' screamed Eve, trying to lift him up off the bike.

'Quick, Clovis, pull him out.' Clovis dragged Uncle Rufus's limp body clear from the cycle and away from the open doors of the machine.

Eve stroked her uncle's cheek. 'Can you hear me?'

Clovis grabbed a bottle of water from his rucksack and brought it to the professor's lips.

His eyelids fluttered and then he moaned. 'What happened?'

'It's all right, Uncle. You're safe now,' said Eve, sitting back on her heels, relief rushing through her.

Uncle Rufus began to mumble, moving his head from side to side.

'Is he dreaming?' she asked Clovis.

Uncle Rufus whispered some more; his voice wasn't clear at first.

'What's he saying?' asked Eve.

Clovis and Eve leaned close to Uncle Rufus's mouth. 'He's here!' he gasped. 'Jack's here, inside Endeavour. The machine couldn't handle his strength, I couldn't get him to the Abyss.

I had to bring him back. He's in the compartment still, but I don't know how long Endeavour can hold him.'

Clovis and Eve looked at each other in terror.

'You must get out, get help, call the inspector,' continued Uncle Rufus, and then he closed his eyes, winced in pain and lost consciousness.

Slowly, Eve and Clovis turned towards Endeavour and with horror saw the shadowy outline of a tall ghostly figure through the smoke. It was twisting and flailing around inside the small see-through compartment. Uncle Rufus had managed to trap the ghost of Jack, all right, but what now?

'Oh my God,' whispered Clovis. 'It's him, Jack the Ripper! He's here.'

Eve screamed. The shock of seeing his ghost was unreal, unfathomable. Clovis watched through the panel as the demonic spirit pressed his translucent face up against the partition wall. His eyes were red, his mouth wide open, and flies spewed out and encircled the small compartment. The infamous black cape fluttered and whipped about, seemingly by some tremendous tornado of energy. Clovis was reminded of an enraged, caged bat.

Jack began to pound on the compartment wall with balled-up gloved fists, each hit harder than the last; then like a deranged creature he began to smash his head into the glass-like panel, all the while never taking his red eyes off Eve. The noise was horrific and terrifying. Suddenly a loud *CRACK!* splintered the barrier. Clovis and Eve gasped out loud, watching in fear as the fracture began to split slowly down the pane.

'We need to get out,' shouted Clovis. He began to haul the unconscious Uncle Rufus towards the stairs. Eve screamed again as she watched the ghost of the Ripper smash against the partition and saw with gut-wrenching dread that the ghost was about to break through.

Eve screamed at Clovis: 'Come on . . . hurry!' They pulled Uncle Rufus's body along the floor as quickly as they could. Alarmingly, a dreadful, heart-stopping sound came from within Endeavour. The compartment holding Jack gave an almighty *SNAP!* The pressure from his energy was too much for the previously unbreakable polythrixium. Jack's spirit grinned malevolently from the other side of the partition. He tapped on the pane slowly with one finger: *tap . . . tap . . . tap*. His diabolical head was tipped to one side and a most hideous smile was stretched across his evil face.

Uncle Rufus was heavy. Eve and Clovis had managed to drag him to the top of the stairs but they weren't quick enough. The pane shattered into a million tiny pieces and Jack walked through the partition. He threw his head back and laughed, a hideous, awful sound that echoed and rattled around the loft room.

They were too late. Eve and Clovis couldn't get Uncle Rufus down the stairs, and the terrifying ghost of Jack the Ripper stomped towards them, never taking his eyes off Eve.

He stood over them like a building crane, his head bent down, his top hat precariously balanced, laughing manically.

Eve and Clovis clung to each other. Shaking and whimpering, they tried to cover Uncle Rufus's body with their own. The Ripper opened his doctor's bag and extracted a long silver medical instrument, the end red-hot with fire, the smell of sulphur burning their nostrils. The whole room seemed to vibrate, and sheets and books began to fly about the small space, the monstrous energy causing chaos all around them. Eve shrieked and buried her head into her uncle's chest as the ghost moved closer. Clovis squeezed his eyes shut, waiting for the end to come.

Then suddenly something ran in front of them. Eve and Clovis looked up to see someone causing Jack's spirit to tumble backwards. Was it Tom? No, they didn't recognise who it was. A man rose up in front of them and faced Jack. Whoever this person was, he had taken the ghost by surprise.

The stranger began to chant some strange, foreign words. Jack snarled and snapped at the man with his pointed yellow teeth but oddly, didn't come any closer. Then the man poured a strange-looking powder onto his open palm, took a huge breath and blew. The powder flew out of his hand and hung in the air for a second, then slowly it floated down like a fine rain, covering the spirit of Jack. The ghost roared, his mouth opened wide, revealing a gaping black monstrous chasm, from which hundreds more black flies flew out. Slowly Eve and Clovis watched as the ghost of Jack the Ripper faded into nothing.

'He's gone,' said Eve breathlessly. 'Oh, my God! He's gone!'

'Not quite,' replied the stranger. He turned around to reveal himself. He was tall and smartly dressed in a waistcoat and crisp white shirt. His sleeves were rolled up, revealing many tattoos that intertwined, covering both his dark arms. His hair was shoulder length, wavy and black, his face was brown and kind, but his most distinguishing features were the two tattoos just under his eyes. Each was of a star and a moon with three wavy lines running diagonally, separating the symbols.

'Forgive my sudden entrance,' he said in a smooth Arabic accent, 'but I think you needed my assistance. Please let me introduce myself. I am Anwaar Albert Saygh, an old friend of the professor's.'

Immediately he went to Uncle Rufus's side, put his arm under his head and then whispered more foreign words close to his ear.

'What are you doing?' asked Eve suspiciously.

'Don't worry, he will be fine. He'll come round,' Anwaar whispered. 'He'll have a terrible headache when he does though.'

CHAPTER 18

Enter a Tall Dark Handsome Stranger

Uncle Rufus moaned loudly, 'What happened?' He opened his eyes and through his blurred vision he saw Eve, Clovis and . . . Anwaar? 'Oh, my dear friend . . . am I dreaming?' he said, not quite believing what he was seeing.

'No, my friend, you are not.' Anwaar smiled down warmly at his old comrade. 'It's me. I've come to help you all.'

Uncle Rufus sat up slowly and immediately wished he hadn't moved, it felt as though a brass band was performing wildly in his head. 'I can't believe it, you're really here. It's so good to see you.' Uncle Rufus went to hug his old friend, but suddenly grimaced with pain.

'Take it easy, Professor,' said Anwaar. 'You've literally had the life sucked out of you.'

'We need to take him home and we need to call the inspector,' said Eve, relieved that her uncle was all right.

'I don't think we'll have enough time for that,' said Anwaar. 'I have a feeling that our friend Jack will be back before long. He is out for revenge.'

'How come you know so much?' asked Clovis, who was

still confused by the sudden arrival of this strange-looking man.

'All will be explained in good time, Clovis, but for now you must trust me and help me get the professor to a safe place.'

'Can't we just take him home?' said Eve, her patience wearing thin.

'No, there's no time. I spoke to your young friend before I came in here.'

'Who? Tom?'

'Yes, the one who was asleep outside. He did a brave thing travelling to the Otherside and saving those ghost children,' said Anwaar.

'Yes,' whispered Uncle Rufus. 'He was definitely brave. But foolish. He went against my wishes. Though I do concede that because of him, the ghost children are with their mother now.'

'Yes, that's good for them but unfortunately that's bad for you,' said Anwaar, standing up.

'What do you mean?' asked Clovis.

'Jack has no victims now, and that's something he can't exist without. I take it he has seen you all, yes?'

'Yes,' replied Eve.

'Well, sadly that means you are his new victims. He will hunt you down.' Anwaar's answer was like a punch to the stomach.

'But, Uncle, you said the ghost of Jack wouldn't be able

to leave the school. Has that changed?' Eve was aware her voice sounded confrontational and tried to calm down. She had been able to cope with the ghosts here but she didn't think she could cope if a ghost followed her home again — they'd had that happen before with their last investigation.

'I think it would be foolish to leave this place,' whispered Anwaar to Uncle Rufus. Then he turned his attention back to Eve and Clovis. 'You can leave, but only when his spirit has been sent to the Abyss, otherwise I can't guarantee the safety of your families.'

'I'm sorry, Anwaar, but who *are* you and how come you know so much about us and this case?' Eve was intrigued but she also was on guard.

'It's all right, Eve,' whispered Uncle Rufus, who was now looking a little better. 'This is the friend I told you about. We worked together at SPI, some years back when Jack's ghost first appeared.'

'Ahh ... You're the man who ... ran off?' said Eve, suddenly looking embarrassed at her choice of words.

'Yes, I am the man who ... disappeared. I went all over the world, researching and training, now I'm back.' Anwaar did a little bow and smiled, revealing a perfect set of white teeth. Eve blushed and looked away, not quite sure what to make of this handsome stranger.

Thudding interrupted everyone. It was coming from the stairs. Footsteps came closer and closer, followed by the sound of snuffling and heavy breathing.

'Oh my God!' said Eve, hiding behind Clovis.

Tom's head popped up at the top of the stairs.

'Tom!' Eve and Clovis rushed to their friend and hugged him. The deep breaths and snuffling were, of course, from a very tired-looking Boris who, upon seeing Uncle Rufus and Anwaar, suddenly became most excited.

'He remembers you, Anwaar,' said Uncle Rufus, stroking his dog.

Anwaar got down on his knees and petted Boris. 'He was only a pup when I last saw him. My, what a beast you have become, my friend.' Anwaar laughed and received a slobbery kiss from the bulldog.

Uncle Rufus stood up but he was still a little shaky. 'Now, I think it's time you all went outside,' he said. 'Anwaar and I have unfinished business to attend to and you chaps *cannot* be here.'

Eve, Tom and Clovis looked relieved. They began to walk towards the stairs when Anwaar spoke.

'I'm afraid that's not possible,' he said. 'They need to stay here with us. At least I can protect them.'

'And how, my dear fellow, do you propose to do that?' asked Uncle Rufus.

'I've spent the last five years training and working as a demonologist. My work is specialising in demons and spirits of a dark nature.'

'Really? Why didn't you tell me? Why didn't you keep in touch?'

'I had my reasons. Let us discuss this later, Professor, for I fear we may not have much more time to prepare. We are safe for now. Jack needs to recharge, he needs more energy, so that gives us a little time, at least.'

Uncle Rufus nodded at his old friend and waved Eve, Clovis and Tom back to him.

Anwaar stared intently at Tom. 'We must all stay together. We don't know if Jack is aware that you, Tom, are the one who sent his little victims into the light.'

Tom was still puzzled by the stranger but nodded in agreement nonetheless.

Uncle Rufus looked at the three friends. 'Now, I want you to listen carefully to Anwaar and do everything he tells you to do. Is that clear?' Eve and Clovis nodded in agreement.

He turned to Tom. 'Tom?' He directed a steely glare at him. Tom looked down at his hands, nodded again, feeling ashamed of his earlier betrayal.

'First things first,' said Anwaar. 'We must go down to the lowest part of the building. I assume there is a cellar?'

'I'm not sure.' Uncle Rufus rubbed his chin.

'There's a cellar, remember,' said Clovis. 'Mr Wilson mentioned that and the loft when he was giving us a tour.'

'Good boy,' said Anwaar. 'Everyone stay close together,' said Anwaar. He and Uncle Rufus walked ahead down the stairs, talking quietly as they went.

'What do you think?' whispered Tom to the others as they followed.

'I like him,' said Eve.

'Yeah, I bet you do,' laughed Clovis, elbowing Eve in the ribs.

'Don't be stupid, not like that. He's a total mystery, though, isn't he? And he saved our lives back there.'

Tom interrupted their whispered conversation. 'I just want to say, I'm so sorry, guys, you know, for running off like that and taking Endeavour.'

The three friends stopped walking and turned to each other. Tom nervously bit his bottom lip and carried on. 'I know it was stupid of me but I just needed to help them. I promised, you see, and they begged and begged inside my head and, well, I . . . know what it's like to miss your mum.' Tom was exhausted and sad. The last thing he needed right now was to lose his two best friends. 'I'm sorry.' He looked down at the floor, shame washing over him.

Eve gave a wry smile. 'You're an idiot but you're forgiven. Don't forget though that I know what it feels like to miss your mum too. You could've come and talked to me about it.'

'I know that, but I didn't want to bring all that stuff up again. That was a terrible time in your life. I wanted to do something to make things better for someone, not worse. You do understand, don't you?'

Eve and Clovis looked at each other quickly, then Eve reached over to Tom, grabbed him and gave him a big hug. 'You're forgiven, but if you do anything like that again, I'll kill you.'

'Yeah, that goes for me too,' said Clovis. 'We were really worried about you. Don't ever be an ass again . . . though that would be almost impossible for you, wouldn't it?' Clovis leaned over to his friend and playfully punched him on the arm.

Tom breathed out a sigh of relief and felt a little better. He hoped Uncle Rufus would be just as understanding. He watched him and the stranger walking in front of them.

'So . . . where did he come from?' he said, nodding at Anwaar. 'I woke up in the car and he was staring at me through the window and he seemed to know my name and everything that had been going on.'

Eve hugged herself and said, 'It was awful, Tom. Jack was about to burn us and do God knows what else—'

Clovis interrupted quickly. 'I honestly thought we were going to die, but then he —' he pointed at Anwaar's back — 'just *appeared* and saved us . . .' He brought his voice down really low and whispered out of the corner of his mouth: '. . . making *you know who* evaporate. It was incredible.'

'And what about the dust he blew into the air? That was awesome,' said Eve, shaking her head in disbelief.

'What does a demonologist do, exactly?' asked Tom. He felt secretly a little relieved he had been in the car but also a bit disappointed that he'd missed out on some of the action.

'Well, it's a person who studies demons and, I assume, knows how to destroy them,' said Clovis. 'Anwaar looks like he knows his stuff. Let's hope he can get rid of Jack once and for all.'

'But why study *demons*? You wouldn't catch me wanting to dabble in all that dark stuff,' said Tom.

By now they had reached a wooden door at the far end of the corridor.

'This might be it; its position is right within the building.' Uncle Rufus turned the handle, and with a little help from Anwaar's shoulder, the door gave way.

'Torches on, chaps, I think we've found the cellar.' Uncle Rufus went down first. Stone steps fell into total darkness.

'Great, the ghost of Jack the Ripper, and a pitch-black cellar, what more could we ask for?' said Tom under his breath.

'Everyone careful,' said Anwaar. 'The steps are slippery.'

The stone stairs twisted around to the right and eventually brought everyone down into a warren of arched brick chambers.

'I think this must have been the storage cellars for the old buildings that used to be here. They must have built the school on top using the original foundations,' said Uncle Rufus, panning his torch around the rooms.

'That makes sense,' said Anwaar, swiping some cobwebs out of the way.

'Where do you want us to go?' Uncle Rufus asked Anwaar.

'The largest room will be best.'

'Why do we need to be in the cellar?' asked Eve, shivering; it was damp and cold down in the darkness.

'You will see,' said Anwaar. 'I need to be as close as possible to the earth.'

Uncle Rufus nodded; Eve, Clovis and Tom looked quizzically at each other.

Everyone followed Anwaar as he inspected each room. Most were bare but some had old tables and chairs stacked high in corners. He stopped dead in the centre of the largest room, turned around slowly, closed his eyes and breathed in steadily.

'This will do,' he said, smiling. He then opened up his smart waistcoat to reveal his shirt was covered with pockets; in each one there was a small object.

Everyone watched, fascinated, as Anwaar took a paper packet out of one of his pockets, ripped it open, then poured some fine, white powder in a wide circle on the ground.

'Everyone, please stand inside the circle.'

They did as Anwaar asked while he marked a five-pointed star out on the stone floor with chalk. At each point he placed a strange, orange-coloured crystal. 'This is also for protection. It is very strong, the stones are incredibly powerful.' Anwaar smiled at Uncle Rufus's inquisitive look. 'All in good time, Professor. Now whatever happens, you must all stay inside the circle of salt. It will protect you against his evil.'

'What about you?' asked Eve, concerned.

'I'm already protected, my markings give me all the help

I need.' Anwaar tapped one of his arms, showing his many intricate tattoos.

Clovis was entranced by this man. He was like something out of the movies.

Tom, on the other hand, was very confused and kept whispering to his friends, 'Is he part of SPI?'

Uncle Rufus placed a protective arm across Tom's shoulders. 'When this is over, young man, we'll talk, but for now you must listen.'

Tom nodded. A flutter of nerves tickled his stomach; he wasn't sure what the professor had in store for him, but he was grateful for his protection. He huddled in closer to the professor. Boris sat on Tom's feet and let out a small gust of warm air. '*Why*, Boris? Why me?' he whispered, rolling his eyes.

'Now,' said Anwaar, 'I must dangle the carrot, as you say. Eve, come here, if you please.'

Eve looked to her uncle, not sure if she should oblige. Uncle Rufus nodded his approval and she rather reluctantly walked out of the circle and stood next to Anwaar.

'Forgive me, Eve, but I fear you are the thing he craves. You are a beautiful young lady and that is like a drug to a spirit like Jack. When I give you the word, you *must* jump back into the circle. Is that understood?' Eve felt her cheeks burn with the compliments. She nodded but inside regretted that she had agreed to be the bait.

Everyone settled down and waited, not sure what they

were about to witness. All of their trust was in Anwaar, a man who Uncle Rufus hadn't seen or heard from for five years, and who had let him down in the past.

Time had been too short for explanations — was it enough to put all their faith in him? Clovis wasn't so sure, Tom hoped so and Eve, well, it looked like she had the most to lose. Uncle Rufus, Clovis and Tom watched from the protection of the circle and Eve stood absolutely still, feeling very vulnerable. She was shaking, clearly terrified.

Uncle Rufus questioned himself again for putting these young people in harm's way. Maybe he wasn't giving them enough credit. Hadn't Tom managed to reunite Annie and Joe with their mother all on his own? He had to admit the lad was brave, that was for sure.

Anwaar shouted out, breaking Uncle Rufus's thoughts.

'He's coming!'

Everyone held their breath, waiting for the terror to begin. They knew what he looked like, knew how strong he was. Was a circle of salt really going to protect them? thought Clovis. He wasn't so sure, in his mind he had a plan, and that was: 'If all else fails, grab everyone and make a run for it'.

Tom didn't know *what* to think. He wasn't sure he was ready for this. He suddenly felt tired again and stumbled backwards. Uncle Rufus grabbed him firmly and held him up.

Anwaar and Eve stood in between the circle and the five-pointed star. No one moved a muscle, not a word was uttered. A single bead of sweat slowly trickled down Anwaar's forehead, and he quickly wiped it away with the back of his hand.

The first sign that Jack had entered the room was the temperature: it dropped so quickly that even the brick walls began to frost over. Everyone's breath formed a small cloud around them. Boris started to growl. Then the floor began to vibrate, lightly at first.

'Can you feel that?' asked Uncle Rufus, looking about him through the white mist of breath.

'Uh huh,' gulped Eve, grabbing hold of Anwaar's arm.

'Yep,' whispered Clovis.

'It's getting stronger,' said Tom, clasping the hem of Uncle Rufus's shirt.

Astonishingly the floor began to move, undulating up and down. The stone cracked, then earth and soil spat upwards like an angry monster taking its first breath. The solid ground they had been standing upon only moments earlier vibrated like an earth tremor while all around them the floor swelled and cracked. Inside the ring of salt, though, the floor remained intact.

Anwaar and Eve stumbled but somehow managed to keep upright. Tom, Uncle Rufus and Clovis had each other to cling to.

'Now, Eve! Get in the circle,' cried Anwaar.

Eve jumped back into the safety of the salt ring, grabbing hold of her friends and Uncle Rufus.

'He's trying to unbalance us. Hold on, stay in the circle,'

shouted Anwaar. The noise was incredible, a roaring, groaning sound.

Then a voice: deep, guttural and fierce. 'You are all mine.'

Uncle Rufus pulled everyone down onto the floor and brought his arms around them protectively. Boris was glued to Tom's foot.

'Look!' cried Eve, pointing to the ceiling. There he was. Jack the Ripper, his evil, twisted, scarred face looked down on them all, red eyes illuminating the room, making everything seem like a blazing inferno.

Anwaar began to chant more strange words. Over and over he repeated his mantra. Faster and faster. He moved back and forth in a trance-like state.

The floor began to slow its sea-like movements, and the noise began to quieten. Jack's face dissolved into nothingness.

'Is that it?' whispered Tom, opening his eyes.

'I don't think so,' answered Uncle Rufus, never taking his eyes off Anwaar's back.

Sure enough, a loud boom reverberated throughout the room, shaking the floor again.

Jack's ghost appeared once more but this time he was a full-bodied apparition. He stood on the far side of the five-pointed-star. In quick succession, he snapped his grotesque mouth open and closed, as if trying to bite through an invisible rope. His black-gloved hands were twisted round now, back to front. His head jerked from side to side, never taking his red eyes off Anwaar. Jack's black cloak fluttered in a breeze of freezing cold air which smelled of sulphur, death and decay. The ghost was becoming more translucent.

'He's getting weaker!' shouted Anwaar. 'Can you see that?'

Suddenly Jack made a move around the five-pointed star. Eve realised with horror that the ghost was trying to get to them . . . to her.

'Stay inside the circle!' commanded Anwaar. 'He can't hurt you; I promise.'

Eve squealed and closed her eyes, not entirely sure whether to believe Anwaar.

The demonologist took something else out of his shirt pocket. It looked like a long white pointed crystal. Everyone watched as he spoke more words, and as he uttered them, he swirled the white crystal around in a circle above the chalk star.

'Oh, my goodness! Will you look at that!' whispered Uncle Rufus.

They stared in astonishment as Anwaar seemingly began to open up a hole in the floor. It was a deep black mass that swirled around in front of the five-pointed star. A whole new dark world had opened up before their eyes.

An unearthly noise echoed around them, and the sounds of anguished screaming circled the room like a hurricane. It was so deafening and desperate, it made Eve feel sick to the stomach.

'What's that?' shouted Clovis.

'That, my dear boy, is an entrance to the Abyss. Though how Anwaar has managed to open it here, I will never know.'

The ghost of Jack the Ripper faltered. He gnashed and clawed at the air, trying desperately to reach the friends in the circle. He couldn't seem to get anywhere near Anwaar, and he was clearly afraid of him. The others watched on, terrified, yet curious to know what their new friend was going to do next.

A sharp current of electricity suddenly shot out of the end of Anwaar's crystal. It caught Jack in his torso, and the screams he made joined the cacophony of souls from inside the black hole. Anwaar began to shake as he used all his strength. But somehow Jack was able to resist the blast of light. How was that possible? This entity was much stronger than Anwaar had first thought. He pulled all of his power and light together and tried one more time to bring the evil creature down. The electricity throbbed through him and travelled down into the crystal.

The others stared on in wonder as all of Anwaar's tattoos began to radiate a bluish bright light that pulsed and vibrated. At last, his power bolted into the spectre, sweeping Jack off his feet in one glorious motion.

Suddenly a beautiful white glow began to emerge next to Anwaar. Where it came from, the observers didn't know, but they could suddenly feel the presence of numerous souls. Slowly the spectral visitors began to show themselves.

Anwaar kept his concentration on Jack, he mustn't be

distracted. The ghost of Jack the Ripper was now on its hands and knees, crawling towards the circle of salt.

'I don't believe it!' cried Tom. 'It's Elizabeth and Lucy, they're all here . . . look, Professor . . . these ghosts, they are all Jack's victims.' Everyone looked on in amazement as the ghosts of ten women and two children hovered in a group to the right of Anwaar. They turned to Tom and smiled, then one by one they formed a line, their bodies gliding with a calm, serene fluidity.

They moved in harmony, together as one, behind Jack. The evil ghost didn't realise what was happening as they circled closer to him. Their strength was Jack's weakness. Together they were formidable; they were the ones who would end his reign of terror. With one sharp, brisk movement, the women and children pushed Jack the Ripper into the black hole of the groaning Abyss. They all watched with tremendous satisfaction as his ghost sizzled and screamed, while disembodied shadowy arms and clawed hands levitated upwards and began to wrench their newest prize down into their demonic pit.

Anwaar dropped to his knees and began to chant again. The black hole, with all its roaring demonic inhabitants, slowly closed up until eventually the cellar's stone floor was once again back in place.

The ghosts of Elizabeth, Lucy, and all the other victims glided over to the salt circle. 'He is no more,' whispered Elizabeth.

Lucy held the hands of Annie and Joe. They smiled and then in shyness hid behind their mother's flowing dress.

Then everyone witnessed the souls of Elizabeth, Lucy, Annie, Joe and all the other victims walk back into the beautiful brilliant white light. Once they had all vanished, the light began to diminish until it was no more.

The room in the cellar went totally dark again; no one said anything. They couldn't. There was so much to say but now wasn't the time. They were all dazed and tired.

Uncle Rufus needed to go back to his attic and download all the data and footage they'd captured. He would like to talk to his old friend, too, and he had to speak to Tom; then they could all discuss the case to finally join the dots. But first things first, Uncle Rufus wanted to go home and put the kettle on.

CHAPTER 19

Explanations and a New Tattoo

Uncle Rufus drove his Mini and all the equipment back, while everyone else walked home with Anwaar. They enjoyed the sun on their faces and the comfortable silence as they strolled along the busy high street. Clovis, Eve and Tom nudged each other and couldn't help but smile as they noticed the curious looks Anwaar was getting from the locals.

Once back at Eve's house, they all made their way up to the attic, knowing it was where Uncle Rufus would be. Sure enough, they found him feeding the memory cards from the night-vision cameras into his computer. Messenger One was already processing the recordings from their EVP watches. Uncle Rufus hadn't wasted any time getting all their footage ready to be analysed.

Anwaar was clearly impressed with Uncle Rufus's attic, and some time was spent explaining the various inventions lying around the room.

'So, what happened, Anwaar, where did you go?' asked Uncle Rufus, gesturing for his friend to sit down on the sofa. The others couldn't wait to hear where this strange exotic man had been for the last five years, and readily plonked themselves down on the floor.

Anwaar refused the invitation to sit and propped himself casually against Uncle Rufus's desk, ankles crossed, arms folded. He leaned slightly back and looked skywards, noticing the twinkling constellations for the first time. His dark eyes widened at the spectacle but he didn't say anything about them.

'After our brush with Jack the first time, Professor, and my failure to overcome his power, I realised I had failed. When I came face to face with Jack, my fear got the better of me, it gripped my very soul. I can't believe I ran out on you and left you to defend yourself against such an evil force. I had shamed myself, the SPI, but most importantly, my friend. I left you there in a cowardly fashion and I couldn't forgive myself.'

'Oh, Anwaar, please, that spirit could break the strongest of people. I was shocked at your departure, but it was understandable.'

'No, it was my own weakness that caused you more danger. I was hot-headed, cavalier. I didn't listen to your instructions.' Anwaar leaned forward and looked at his enraptured young audience. 'I secretly thought that if I could dispose of the Ripper's spirit, then it would give me status, something that I longed for. I'm afraid and embarrassed to say I secretly had a rather large ego and that, my dear friends, can be a destructive thing. Ultimately, as I found to my distress, that can lead you to some very dark places. All my life, I only ever wanted to be good at *something*, and after convincing myself that I could be the greatest ghost hunter, I threw myself headlong into a frightening situation that I wasn't equipped for.'

Uncle Rufus put his hand on Anwaar's back. 'My dear fellow, I had no idea you had all those feelings. I wish you had spoken to me; I would have understood. No one ever thought you had a big ego; you were always quiet and respectful.'

Anwaar smiled at his friend and sighed. 'These feelings, I kept buried deep down but all the time they were pulling me apart. It was like a little devil had entered my soul. I didn't like the man I was becoming. Failing in my attempt to destroy Jack's ghost, and running out on you, filled me with nothing but shame and remorse. Putting you at risk like that made me realise that enough was enough. I decided I had to rid myself of this thing that was blackening my spirit. I travelled around the world, enriching my soul and learning humility. While on my many adventures, I discovered a village deep in the deserts of Iran. The people there lived by the old ways, and they taught me many incredible things. There I was educated in the art of demonology by an ancient and very wise master. Professor, the things I've seen . . . you would not believe them. I spent a few years living with that master and learning his craft.'

'Did he give you those tattoos?' asked Clovis, mesmerised by Anwaar's story.

'Incredible as this sounds, the Otherside placed them on me. I gained each one after I had successfully fought and disposed of a demon. A new one will appear soon.'

'No?!' said Eve, awestruck.

'So, what brought you back here?' asked Uncle Rufus.

'I knew Jack's spirit would escape Highgate Cemetery sooner rather than later. The binding spell that you and the inspector placed on him wasn't strong enough. The inspector contacted me as soon as she heard he was back. She knew I had undertaken demonology training and she thought I might be able to help once the ghosts of the children were dealt with.'

'Ah, so *you* were the demonologist she mentioned.'

'Indeed. She knew straight away that you could both be in danger, as you were the ones who bound him to the grave at Highgate. As we know only too well, Jack loved revenge. She asked me to watch you and make sure that you, Eve and your assistants —' he gestured to Tom and Clovis — 'came to no harm.'

'So you were the one that I kept seeing, following us?' asked Uncle Rufus.

'Yes, I'm sorry about that, but the inspector didn't want you to be alarmed. She was very aware that you wanted to try one last time by yourself. I wanted to help you sooner, but the inspector told me to hang back and so, my friend,

I did.' Anwaar shifted his position, looking a little uncomfortable at his confession.

Suddenly an app on Uncle Rufus's laptop started ringing, signalling that someone was trying to video call.

'Speak of the Devil,' said Uncle Rufus, chuckling at his own pun. He sprang over to his desk and brought his laptop to the sofa. Everyone crowded round as Detective Inspector Rutherford's face beamed from the screen. 'Well, hello everyone!' she shouted. The inspector's voice was loud and excited. 'Glad to see you there too, Anwaar. I believe your case has been successful?'

'Indeed, it has,' said Uncle Rufus. 'Although if it hadn't been for Anwaar, I'm not sure what we would have done.' He smiled warmly at his friend.

'I hope you don't mind that I sent reinforcement, but I suspected Jack was going to be a hard nut to crack, and the SPI didn't want any harm to come to you,' said the inspector.

Uncle Rufus grinned at his long-time friend and colleague. He should have known that she'd take every precaution possible to protect him and his young students.

'Well, you were right,' he said, 'he *was* a hard nut to crack. And I'm grateful for your assistance. I'm afraid I have more work to do on Endeavour though, if it is to transport spirits to the Abyss.'

Detective Inspector Rutherford nodded. 'Ah yes, Endeavour. I've also been made aware of Tom's extraordinary bravery using that astonishing machine. Thank you, Tom. I understand you have reunited two young souls with their mother's spirit.'

Tom looked down bashfully.

'I will need a separate report from you about what you saw on the Otherside. You realise you're the first living human we have on record who's ever been there, breathed the air and walked in its atmosphere *and* returned.'

Clovis and Eve clapped their friend on the back. But Tom felt uncomfortable, considering he had taken the professor's invention and nearly got himself killed. He coughed, conscious of Uncle Rufus's eyes on him. But the inspector hadn't finished.

'At the beginning of this investigation, Tom, you questioned whether you had the skills to be part of the SPI. But you have proved over the last few days that you have a keen sense of empathy and an ability to communicate with the dead. Quite outstanding in someone so young. However, Tom . . .' The inspector's demeanour suddenly changed and she leaned further forward towards the screen.

Tom's head shot up nervously.

'. . . I do believe the professor needs to have a little private chat with you. As far as the SPI is concerned, you can never pull a stunt like that again, young man. There can be no place here for investigators who behave recklessly and don't listen to their instructors.'

Tom's face had gone the brightest shade of red, shame and embarrassment oozing from every pore. He hung his head, his fringe flopping over his eyes.

'I'm sorry,' he mumbled.

'Luckily for you,' continued Detective Inspector Rutherford, 'things turned out all right, but they could have been very different. I'm letting you off with a warning this time, but there will be no second chances. Do I make myself clear?'

Tom nodded and breathed out a sigh of relief.

'Thank you, Inspector Rutherford, and I'm truly sorry for what I did. I will never betray your trust again.' Tom looked at Uncle Rufus shyly and hoped that he knew he was sincere.

'Very well. Now,' said the inspector, changing the subject, 'you must all come here tomorrow for lunch. I think it's important for us to have a debrief. Will the footage be ready for viewing and analysis by then, Professor?'

'Yes, I'm downloading it all as we speak. I'll bring it over to you and I shall be bringing Endeavour too. I think it's for the best,' said Uncle Rufus.

'Wonderful, we can't wait to hear all about it. And, Anwaar, we're expecting you too. We need to celebrate today's victory and close the case. We are all very impressed with everyone's hard work and incredible bravery. Now . . .' The inspector looked behind her and patted her grey curly hair. 'I'm afraid I must away, as Cedric is causing trouble again in the ladies' loos . . . I've been told it has something to do with a blocked-up U-bend and a meat and potato pie.' She rolled her eyes and waved. 'Goodbye, and see you tomorrow, one p.m. sharp. Oh, and Rufus? Get that arm seen to.' Her image disappeared and the screen went blank.

'How come she knows everything?' asked Eve. 'She doesn't miss a trick, does she?'

'She's an incredible woman, eyes and ears everywhere,' replied Anwaar. Suddenly he surprised everyone as he grabbed Uncle Rufus's arm. He rolled the sleeve of his shirt up. 'Relax, Professor, this will not hurt, but I have to take away the mark of the Beast, otherwise you will be for ever tortured.' He opened up his waistcoat once more and took out another small packet. 'Hold still, now.' He sprinkled a fine blue powder over Uncle Rufus's arm. In an instant the strange substance began to fizz and smoke.

'Oh, wow,' whispered Clovis. 'What would have happened if the burn stayed as it was?'

Anwaar looked uncomfortable for a moment. He glanced to Uncle Rufus, who nodded that it was OK to talk. The exchange didn't go unnoticed by Eve. 'If the mark is left on the body, the professor could become one of them, a living demon. Most times, they look and sound like us, they walk amongst us, but are in fact the Devil's puppets, doing his bidding and creating untold damage around the world.'

All three of the friends spoke at once, not quite believing what they were hearing.

'Are you serious?' asked Eve, stunned.

'No way!' exclaimed Tom, his mouth opening and closing like a caught fish.

'Mmmm, fascinating,' murmured Clovis, leaning in closer to look at Uncle Rufus's sizzling arm.

Uncle Rufus spoke quickly. 'And all of that is for another day, chaps.' The colour had drained from his face; he was beginning to feel exhausted and a little uncomfortable.

Anwaar smiled. He took out his long white crystal and began to wave it slowly over his friend's arm, all the while chanting some words so quietly that no one could hear exactly what he said.

'Look!' cried Eve.

Everyone stared at Uncle Rufus's arm, watching in amazement as the mark of the figure of eight and the cross changed into an Egyptian eye.

'What does *that* mean?' asked Eve, worried again.

'No need to be fearful, Eve, this is the Eye of Horus. It will protect him from evil and give him good health.'

'Wow, Uncle, you've got a permanent tattoo.' Eve laughed at her uncle's face. He looked a little miffed.

'Well, I never thought I would get a tattoo, certainly not at my age.' He smiled weakly, not wanting Anwaar to think him ungrateful.

Anwaar shrugged. 'It's better than the alternative, my friend, believe me. Now forgive me, but I must go to pray and give thanks.'

Uncle Rufus and the others followed him to the door,

intending to bid their new friend goodbye. Anwaar held up his hand and grinned, crinkling his strange facial tattoos.

'I shall eat and sleep well, as should you all. I am looking forward to the future and to our many adventures together. Until tomorrow ... *sadeek*.' Anwaar then placed his hands together in a prayer position, closed his eyes and bowed.

'Goodbye, my friend,' said Uncle Rufus, rubbing his new tattoo.

'Bye,' murmured Eve, copying Anwaar's gesture.

'Bye,' said Clovis and Tom, not quite sure what to do.

'What did he just say?' whispered Tom.

'It's Arabic, it means *friend*,' Clovis whispered back, smiling.

Eve turned to her uncle. 'You knew what that burn meant, didn't you?'

'Yes, I knew I only had a short amount of time. I was going to go to SPI to get it sorted. I promise.' Uncle Rufus hugged Eve to him and she hugged him back and let it go.

'Hang on a minute, what about Mr Wilson? He had the burn mark too. We must warn him,' said Clovis, starting to panic.

'It's all right, the inspector has arranged for Mr Wilson to have his removed tomorrow morning, first thing.'

CHAPTER 20

Apologies and New Beginnings

While everyone waited for the footage to finish downloading, they ate fish and chips in the front room. The atmosphere was a relaxed one but there was still a burning issue that was yet to be addressed. Once everyone had finished their meal, the teenagers began to clear up the plates. Boris followed them out to the kitchen, saliva drooling from his chops, a sign he hoped that someone would give him a leftover chip or two.

'Tom, can I have a word, please?' said Uncle Rufus seriously.

Eve and Clovis looked at each other, knowing that Tom was about to have a good talking to. Eve wanted her uncle to go easy on her friend. His situation at home had led him to act out of character, he hadn't been thinking straight at all and his stupidity had nearly cost him his life. Eve believed her uncle would be reasonable . . . well, she hoped he would be.

Tom gave his plate to Eve, and she mouthed, *It'll be all right*, and closed the door behind her. Tom's heart was in his mouth, he fidgeted with his hands, realising they had suddenly become quite sweaty with nerves. He sat down on the edge of the sofa, his back straight, eyes down.

'Now, you know what you did was wrong, don't you, Tom?' said Uncle Rufus. The professor sat forward in his armchair, elbows resting on his knees. Tom was surprised at his tone. He didn't sound angry, well, not yet, any way.

'Yes, of . . . course,' he stammered, 'and I'm so, so sorry. I know I betrayed everyone's trust. I feel so bad about it but I can't explain it. I felt like I knew what Annie and Joe were going through, you know, missing their mum and all, and they kept begging me and pleading.' Tom rubbed his palms over his knees, back and forth, back and forth. He was so stressed right now.

'I know you're a good lad, Tom. I've known you since you were tiny. But I never, ever thought you would do anything as stupid and dangerous as that. You know that you could've been killed, don't you?'

Tom nodded and felt his cheeks burning. He would do anything to make it up to the professor, he hated that he had put himself in this position.

Uncle Rufus shifted in his chair and raked his fingers through his hair. His kind eyes blazed with intensity at Tom. The boy suddenly looked so small, so defenceless. Uncle Rufus felt a pang of sadness as his heart went out to the lad, who was going through such a bad time at the moment.

Uncle Rufus stood up with a sigh and placed his hands in his pockets.

'Tom, what the inspector said is correct. You *do* have a gift for communicating with the dead. And I want to help you harness and develop that gift. But I need you to promise me and the others that you will never do anything like that again, do you understand? I love you like a son and it would kill me if I had to ask you to leave us. I think you have such great potential to be anything you want to be in life, even a great ghost hunter. If you desire it.'

Tom looked up and stared at the professor. Tears threatened to spill from his cheeks. 'I will never disappoint you again, Professor, I promise.'

Uncle Rufus pulled Tom up from the sofa. 'Come here,' he said, and to Tom's surprise, the professor hugged him. 'It's all right, lad,' said Uncle Rufus gently. 'Everything will be all right, you'll see.'

'But the thing is, I won't be able to continue as a ghost hunter,' said Tom. 'I'm moving, you see, to Leeds, to be with my mum.'

Uncle Rufus stared in shock. 'When was this decided? Does Eve know?'

'Yeah, she knows, but I really hoped it wouldn't happen and my mum left me a message about it last night. Looks like we're definitely leaving.'

'Well, that is a great loss to the SPI, I can tell you.'

A sudden knock at the front door interrupted them, and

Tom and Uncle Rufus could hear Eve asking someone to come in. She popped her head round and whispered, 'Tom, there's someone here to see you. In the kitchen.'

Tom looked at Uncle Rufus in confusion — who would come over to Eve's house to see him? When he opened the kitchen door, he nearly collapsed with shock. His mum and dad were standing together in the room.

'Mum!' cried Tom, and he ran to her. All his pent-up emotions and frustrations came flooding out and instantly he burst into tears. He was overjoyed to see her. Relief washed over him as he hugged her hard.

'Oh, Tom, I've missed you,' whispered Angela. Her boy. She had felt so alone without him.

'Hello, son.' Tom's dad interrupted their reunion. Angela gently pushed Tom back but still held onto his hand. A man who Tom hardly recognised walked closer to him: his dad looked very strange, unfamiliar and awkward. He stood, shifting his weight from foot to foot and miraculously, he was wearing a smart suit and tie. His hair was cut short and neatly brushed.

'What's going on?' asked Tom, standing back and looking very confused.

'Sit down, son,' said his dad. He placed his finger in the top of his collar and pulled at it, trying to prise the stiff, uncomfortable material away from his wide neck. 'Me and your mum have decided to give it another go.'

Tom's stomach dropped to the floor. This wasn't what he'd

been expecting. He didn't want to go back into that house and live with that man. He needed his mum and that was all. He hadn't missed his dad for a moment. He'd stopped missing him years ago.

Angela sensed that this news wasn't what Tom wanted to hear and she jumped in nervously. 'I've told your dad that things cannot stay the same,' she said, looking at Dad. He stared down at the kitchen table. Was that *shame* Tom saw on his dad's face? Not possible, surely? 'I've told him,' she continued, 'there's to be no more of his old ways. He's going to get himself sorted out, get back to being the man he was. If he doesn't, I've said that we will go and live somewhere else. Though not with your auntie, that's for sure.' Angela looked uncomfortable for a moment; she had obviously not had a good time in Leeds.

Dad cleared his throat and looked at his son. 'I'm sorry, Tom, sorry for the way I've been with you and your mum.'

Tom's mouth fell open.

'It's no excuse, I know,' continued Dad, 'but after the army, I've not been the same. I saw things over there that I can't get out of my head. And, well, I've, I'm . . .' Again he looked embarrassed and fiddled with the end of his tie, which had flopped down over the table. He rolled it up and down, a motion that seemed to help him as he talked. 'I've arranged to see someone, a counsellor, like. I think it's going to help.' Dad smiled weakly at his son. 'I can change. I know I can. I want to be the man I used to be.

I've even joined a gym. Can you believe that?' He laughed awkwardly.

Tom didn't know what to think. He just couldn't believe it. Was this really his dad? Was it the same man?

'Please, Tom, just give me a chance. I know I've not been a great dad or husband in the last few years.' He took Angela's hand in his and squeezed it. 'I know I've got a lot of making up to do but I promise you, you won't regret it.' Then to Tom's horror, his dad's eyes filled with tears. 'I love you and your mum and I've missed you both these last few days.'

'Now, now, Dan,' said his mum, rubbing his back.

Tom wasn't sure what to do. But he thought of Uncle Rufus and the inspector, and his own recent behaviour. Everyone deserved a second chance. He'd been given his, why shouldn't his dad have one? Suddenly he stood up, went over to his dad and shook his hand. 'OK then, let's give it a go.'

For the first time in recent memory, his dad bear-hugged him.

'You won't regret it, son.'

After Tom had arranged to stay over at Eve's one more night to give his mum and dad some space, he watched them leave the house. As they walked down the steps, his dad stuck his hand out for his mum to take and Tom watched in astonishment as they walked away like loved-up teenagers.

Tom closed the door and leaned against it, not quite sure what he had just witnessed.

'Are you all right?' asked Eve, coming up behind him.

'That was the most bizarre thing I think I've ever seen. Never mind the ghost of Jack the Ripper, I've just seen my dad in a suit, holding my mum's hand and apparently he's cooking lasagne for her dinner.'

Mr Pig wolf-whistled then screeched out, 'Lasagne. My arse!'

CHAPTER 21

The Teacher and the Beast

Mr Wilson, the deputy head of Whitechapel Primary School, didn't know where he was going, or why he felt compelled to leave his family. He just knew that it was the right thing to do.

He had been enjoying dinner with his wife when without warning his arm began to burn again. He'd excused himself and gone up to the bathroom. Running cold water into the sink, Mr Wilson had bathed his arm. But no amount of cold water or burn remedies would ever soothe this injury. He looked up into the bathroom cabinet mirror and ran his hand over his stubbly face. He noticed the dark circles under his red, tired eyes. He was exhausted. Maybe it was the sun that was causing his fatigue. He had been trying to relax in the garden all day but the heat had been too intense for him. He stared at his reflection in the mirror, feeling old and weary. The burn mark still hurt but didn't seem as intense.

Suddenly he heard a voice. He whipped around, it sounded so close to his ear. There it was again! Someone was saying his name, whispering, calling to him. His name, *Kevin*, never sounded so good, the sound was like chocolate, so smooth, so velvety. The word rolled about in his head, *KEVIN, KEVIN,* over and over again. Then it whispered oh-so quietly, *Come to me.* It was hypnotic, that voice. It was as if it were all he needed in his life. He had to go. Had to leave this place.

And so Mr Wilson sneaked down the stairs, stepping over various toys and cuddly animals that his young children had been playing with. Little did he know that he would never see them again. He watched the back of his wife leaning over the sink, singing happily to herself as she washed the dishes.

Like a zombie, Mr Wilson's head could only hear the voice of his master, his reason for being. He automatically picked up the car keys from the bowl on the sideboard and quietly opened the front door. It was dark now, the moon cast its silver glow over the empty suburban street. Without pausing, Mr Wilson robotically opened the car door, started the engine and backed the car out of the drive.

He headed out of the city and eventually sped onto the motorway. Tiredness was not an issue: he felt alive, he hadn't felt like this for years. He was propelled by something, some energy he didn't understand. As he passed the other cars on the motorway, he didn't give what he was doing a second thought, or indeed think of where in the country he was driving. His eyes stared, bulbous, veins red and throbbing, the pupils dilated. The car in front wasn't going fast enough, so he flashed his headlights, urging it to get out of the way.

His knuckles were white with grim determination as he gripped the steering wheel; perspiration trickled down his back. A longing so deep, so ancient, began to rise up into his throat and without warning he roared, his voice enraged like a wild beast, his mouth stretched wide open, spittle flying through the air, landing on the dashboard and windscreen.

After another two hundred miles, Mr Wilson eventually pulled off the motorway. Taking a slip road, he drove until the surrounding area grew more remote. Only blackness surrounded him now as he brought the car to a stop.

The voice in his head was so loud now, he grabbed his head and screamed out with the pain of it. He opened the car door and threw himself out. He left the door open and the car running as he stumbled out into a deserted, barren wilderness. It was a moor. Big boulders and grey rocks scattered the lumpy, black land. Not a soul in sight.

No lights could be seen in the distance as Mr Wilson began to walk into the bleak darkness. Like a possessed animal he tore off his tie and violently ripped at his shirt, throwing the shredded material onto the wild and withered ground. He roared again, but this time it was in pain. Looking down at his arm, the branded tattoo blazed red hot; it throbbed and sizzled as his infected blood hissed through his body.

Mr Wilson slumped down against a boulder. The coolness of the stone soothed his aching limbs just for a few moments. Then abruptly the appalling pain rushed through his body with an obscene rage of energy. He fell forwards onto all fours and saw to his horror that his hands had begun to change shape, change form, into something unearthly. Claws, sinew and bone grew to a disproportionate size. Mr Wilson threw his head back. He was sure it would explode at any moment, the pain and agony were too much to bear.

His whole body transformed in a way that was only heard of in legends and supernatural tales.

His face and head were now that of an enormous, indescribable beast, its teeth so large and sharp. His body rippled with new-grown muscles, he was huge, hairy and taut and his legs were that of a monstrous great wolf, long and lean.

Mr Wilson was no more. He stood up, all fourteen feet of him, threw back his ginormous head and howled at the silvery moon. The hideous monster looked about, and sniffed in the still night, trying to pick up a scent. Then, with another loud, baying cry, he flung himself down onto his front paws and thundered away into the dark wilderness.

Bodmin Moor now had a new beast. *This* beast wasn't a big cat, but a far more dangerous one, and a lot, lot larger. On this moonlit night, a lone werewolf had arrived on the moor. It stalked and prowled, waiting in the shadows for a victim. Little did anyone know that this huge, terrifying, ravenous creature had once been a primary school teacher from Whitechapel, London.

ACKNOWLEDGEMENTS

Thank you to my wonderful soul mate and husband, Karl. You really are my other half.

Thank you to my beautiful daughter Mary for listening to all my ideas and being my best girly friend.

Much gratitude to Debbie Gayle, the real Claudette! Thank you for the inspiration.

Thank you to Charlie Sheppard, my editor, for loving my spooky world. Chloe Sackur, my copy editor, thank you for all your help and suggestions. Paul Black and Rob Farrimond, for all the fun and laughter and of course all your amazing hard work, and Jenny Hastings for the most amazing book covers. I'm in awe! Finally, thank you to all at Andersen Press for making my writing experience such a happy and joyous one. You really are the best.

Yvette Fielding was the youngest ever *Blue Peter* presenter at age eighteen, and she's since gone on to host and produce *Ghosthunting With . . .* and *Most Haunted*. After years of studying ghosts, she's become television's 'first lady' of the paranormal. She lives with her husband and two children in Cheshire.

Yvette's experiences of the paranormal

As in book one of The Ghost Hunter Chronicles, I used some of my own experiences from investigating the paranormal.

I was always under the impression that ghosts couldn't harm you, but oh, how wrong I was.

You'd think that the burns that are inflicted upon Mr Wilson and Uncle Rufus were made up in my head, but not so. I witnessed this horrendous phenomenon for myself while filming an investigation for my TV show, *Most Haunted*.

The location was a normal, small modern house that was positioned in the middle of a large housing estate in Leeds, Yorkshire. The ghost that was believed to haunt the building was allegedly a violent and vicious entity. I remember investigating the downstairs of the house while two crew members, Karl and Stuart, were filming above. Suddenly I heard screaming, followed by a large bang. We ran upstairs as quickly as we could, only to discover one of the expensive film cameras upside down on the floor and Karl and Stuart holding their arms in agony.

'It felt like something whipped me,' said Karl.

Both men had identical long deep red burn marks that wrapped around their forearms. We were all deeply shocked and couldn't wait to leave the place. The burns caused scars on both Karl and Stuart's arms, and can still be seen clearly today.

This phenomenon really intrigued me, and so I began to do lots of research. I discovered that this kind of paranormal activity is only associated with very negative spirits and in all those cases throughout history, burn marks, scratches and cuts feature heavily.

So, if someone tells you that ghosts can't harm you . . . they can, and have done for centuries.

The ghosts of children have always fascinated me, and at the same time have probably scared me the most. I think it's because they are more playful and love nothing more than to be naughty and try to scare you.

There are two spirits of children that live in my house. Their names are Elizabeth and Benjamin, who both lived in the building during the eighteenth century. Elizabeth is nine and Benjamin is seven.

When we first moved into our house, it became apparent rather quickly that we were not on our own. The first thing that started to happen daily was a knocking on the front door. Time after time I would go to answer it, and find there was no one there.

Then the giggling and laughter began. It would happen in the day, when my two children were at school, so I knew then that we had more children living with us, who were not of this realm.

Elizabeth and Benjamin loved to move pieces of furniture, particularly our kitchen chairs. In the morning I would go downstairs to get breakfast ready, but every time I found it was a struggle, as I couldn't open the door. After a fight, I always managed to open the door only to discover that one of the wooden chairs had been pushed up against it.

One Christmas we asked the two ghostly children what they would like as a present. Using the tapping board, they spelled out that they would like a ball and a doll. So off I went and purchased a small football and a doll. I placed them under the Christmas tree with the other presents and hoped that they would both disappear.

Every day I checked and to my disappointment the wrapped presents hadn't moved at all. When it was time to take the tree down, I reached underneath and picked up the two presents, discovering that the parcels were both incredibly light in weight. Karl urged me to open them, and you can imagine our astonishment when we discovered that there was nothing inside the paper. No doll or ball. The paper hadn't been touched at all, and to this day we have never seen the two toys since.

During my investigation of the wonderful ship the *Queen Mary*, I was totally gobsmacked when my team and I discovered a set of wet footprints. They were found by the side of the indoor pool, but the pool had not a drop of water in it.

We took the water and tested it, and to our confusion the water was full of sea salt.

No one else had been in that part of the ship; and how did a pair of small bare feet make two perfectly formed footprints when there was no water around? To this day, it baffles me.

And finally . . . a piano playing on its own.

I've experienced this phenomenon a few times, and fortunately in one case, my fellow investigators managed to capture the evidence on camera at Haden Hill House in Cradley Heath, West Midlands.

We had a film camera positioned in the room where the piano was located and left it rolling all day. When we watched the footage back in the edit, we were amazed to see one key being pushed down, as if an unseen finger was pushing the white key down, and at the same time the eerie sound of the note could be heard echoing around the empty room.

Later that night, the piano played again, the same one note.

I keep waiting for a concerto, but I think I'll be waiting for a long time.

THE
HOUSE
IN THE
WOODS

YVETTE FIELDING

When Clovis, Eve and Tom decide to play with a ouija board in an old abandoned house on Halloween, none of them foresees the horrors they're about to unleash. What starts out as a bit of fun, soon transcends into something far more terrifying when a distressed and determined spirit follows them home. Before long the friends are caught up in a series of events beyond their wildest imaginings and their journey as ghost hunters begins . . .

'When I grow up I wanna be a ghost hunter!'
KEITH LEMON

'If you're reading this scary book in bed then it might be wise to leave the landing light on'
PAUL O'GRADY